A HUNTER BROTHERS CHRISTMAS

M. S. PARKER

BELMONTE PUBLISHING, LLC

Copyright © 2018 Belmonte Publishing LLC

Published by Belmonte Publishing LLC

READING ORDER

Thank you so much for reading A Hunter Brothers Christmas. All books in the Hunter Brothers series can be read stand-alone, but if you'd like to read the complete series, I recommend reading them in this order:

1. His Obsession
2. His Control
3. His Hunger
4. His Secret
A Hunter Brothers Christmas

ONE
CHESTER "CT" HUNTER

DECEMBER 23ʳᵈ, 1984

New York City

I trudged through the gray slush, head bent against the freezing rain, mentally cursing myself for not hailing a cab. I didn't mind taking the subway, but I hated the walk from the station to my office on days like today.

Things were supposed to clear up in a couple hours and the temperature would even out, which meant my after-work walk wouldn't be nearly so miserable, but even that thought couldn't coax a smile. I normally loved this time of year, but for some reason, I wasn't looking forward to Christmas the way I usually did.

A sigh escaped as I reached *The New York Times* building. I'd wanted to work here from the time I was old enough to realize what it meant to be a reporter.

Granted, I was only an intern, but my double BA in communication and English from NYU had given me the status of being a paid intern. I planned on working my ass off with the goal of being a junior reporter by this time next year.

At Thanksgiving, my father had asked how things were going at work. If I hadn't known better, I would've thought he had a genuine interest. Although, I guess, technically, his interest in my answer was genuine, just not for the reasons I wished.

Manfred Hunter was the only child of an only child from one of Boston's finest and oldest families. He wasn't simply old money though. He had the same business savvy that had allowed our ancestors to weather the ups and downs of the economy successfully. I'd never asked how much we were worth because I'd never wanted to know. Knowing would have only increased the pressure on me to follow in my father's footsteps and head up the family business.

I breathed a sigh of relief as I stepped into the warm lobby and stomped my feet on the rug. One of my fellow interns came in just behind me, shivering from head to toe despite the massive coat hanging on his lanky frame. A scarf was wrapped almost completely around his face, but I knew who it was all the same. Only one guy at the office bundled up like that when it wasn't below zero.

"Looking good, Finn," I said as I waited for him to remove his scarf and dig through the layers to find his ID. "I have to ask, what do you plan on doing when the wind chill's low enough to freeze the snot on your face?"

"That's disgusting," Argus Finn said, his voice surprisingly delicate as he scrunched his nose. "You don't understand. You grew up in Boston. I'm a Southern gentleman." He drawled the last few words, as if his Georgian heritage was in any doubt.

I shook my head, laughing. I got along with most of the staff, but Finn and I had really hit it off when he started at the paper a month after me. Though he hadn't come out and said anything specific to me, I knew he was gay. A lot of the people at the paper did too, but no one made it into a thing. They didn't go overboard to welcome him either though. Maybe that was why the two of us got along so well. Not that I was gay, but because my co-workers treated me differently because of who my family was and where I came from. The moment they'd figured it out, everyone had suddenly become painfully polite. Finn, however, matched me word for sarcastic word.

We both flashed our IDs at the security guard who barely glanced at them before waving us through. One day, I was going to swap IDs with someone and see if the guard noticed. The way the world was going, security measures would soon become tighter, not more lax.

"Were you serious about how cold it was going to get?" Finn asked as we got onto the elevators. "Seriously, dude, will it?"

"Did you just 'seriously, dude' me?" I laughed. "And yes, it's going to get that cold. Didn't you bother to check what the weather was like before moving here?"

"It's the *New York Times*. It's been my first pick since I realized I wanted to be a journalist. I would've gone to Alaska if it meant I could write for them."

"I know what you mean," I said. "I love being able to say that I work for the *Times*."

"Even if work is all you do?" Finn asked as we stepped off the elevator.

Interns and junior reporters had their own desks on this floor, even if we were crammed in like sardines. We didn't get our own computers, of course, especially not the interns, but a couple of the financial guys said there was a good chance that the cost of computers would keep coming down until it was common for everyone to have them. As it was, we had a few for us to share if we weren't working with a specific senior reporter on a story. Personally, I preferred an old-fashioned notebook.

"We both work crazy hours," I said as I draped my coat over the back of my chair.

"I work my schedule," Finn countered, unwrapping himself from his multiple layers. "You come into work even when you don't have to."

I shrugged. He wasn't wrong. My internship paid a meager salary with a set number of hours, and it didn't make room for overtime. When I came in on my own time, I didn't get paid for it, but I wasn't in it for the money. I was proving something. To myself. To the rest of the staff.

To my father.

"Don't you want to have a life?" Finn asked, taking his seat at the desk next to mine. "I mean, I'm all for being passionate about what you do, but we can't only live and breathe work."

"Can't we?"

Finn rolled his eyes. "You need to have some fun, CT. You do know what fun is, right?"

"I have fun," I argued. "Just because I don't go out to bars and–"

"There's a party tonight," Finn cut in. "I have a cousin who has a friend in the Hamptons, and they're throwing a big holiday bash. You should come with me because my cousin is perfect for you."

I held up a hand. "Whoa. There's a big difference between a party and a set up."

"Not a set up," Finn said, his thin shoulders shrugging up to his ears. "More like a blind date."

"You want me to go to a party tonight to meet your cousin for a blind date." I wondered if it sounded as crazy to hear as it did to say.

Finn's head bobbed up and down. "I think the two of you will really hit it off."

"That's what you said about the last girl you tried to fix me up with," I reminded him. "She wanted to know when I was going to write about her acting career taking off."

Finn winced. "Veronica was a mistake."

I raised an eyebrow. "And what about the one before her? Bianca, I think her name was. She grabbed my dick through my pants."

Finn grinned at me and leaned back in his chair, dark eyes dancing. "That just sounds like a good time to me."

"We were at a hockey game," I countered. "There were kids around."

Finn held his hands up in surrender. "Okay, so maybe I've picked a couple bad ones."

"A couple?" An idea occurred to me. "How about you and I make a deal, Finn? I'll go with you tonight, meet your cousin, and you promise me that she's the last one you try to set me up with."

The front legs of Finn's chair thumped down on the floor, and he stuck out his hand. "Deal. But if you end up liking my cousin, you give me your next story."

"All right," I agreed as I shook his hand.

I didn't bother to tell him that it wasn't going to happen. Not because I wouldn't honor the bet if he won, but because there was no way in hell I'd ever fall for Finn's cousin. First, because I wasn't looking for love, and second, because Finn had the shittiest taste in, well, men and women alike.

I'd go tonight and meet Finn's cousin, and then I'd never have to listen to him nag me about dating again. Not that he wouldn't nag me about other things, but that was fine with me. I didn't mind the friendly picking about stupid stuff. I just wanted his hands off my lack of a love life. If I was meant to be with someone, then I'd find them. It was that simple.

TWO
ABIGAIL SLADE

DECEMBER 23RD, 1984

New York City

Having lived in Seattle, Washington for years, I was used to the perpetual damp. Portland, Oregon hadn't exactly been an arid place to grow up either. Neither city could compare to New York when it came to freezing my ass off though. I liked the cold, even when it was slushy and gross. I always had, even when I had to go out in it. There was something about bundling up and walking in the fresh but dreary air that I enjoyed.

I pulled my winter coat more tightly around me and wished I would've remembered to bring something warmer than my scrubs to walk home in. Technically, as a volunteer at the hospital, I wasn't required to wear scrubs, but I was majoring in nursing at NYU and knew that scrubs were the best way to avoid staining regular clothes with blood and other...things. It made the most sense to just start wearing them now.

The walk from the hospital to the subway, then from the subway to my dorm on Broome Street, wasn't a bad one, and it helped me stay in shape. A lot of people didn't realize what a physical occupation nursing was.

I sighed as I remembered the last time I'd gone to the gym. Usually, I got at least a couple hours in a week, but my finals this past semester had been brutal as I'd been finishing up some of my non-nursing requirements. Instead of doing some lifting and running, I'd spent most of my time trying to understand *The Color Purple* and figuring out the connections between the American and French Revolutions. I had an appreciation for history, but no love for being required to memorize it.

"Abigail!" My roommate shouted as she threw open the lobby door. "Get your skinny ass in here! It's cold as hell!"

I'd never understood that phrase. Wasn't hell supposed to be hot? If that was the case, how could something be as *cold* as hell?

"What are you doing down here wearing just *that*?" I gestured at her pajamas and fuzzy koala slippers. "No wonder you're cold." I stepped past her.

"I've been waiting for you, like, *forever*."

Griselda Viesturs was nineteen, like me, and also a nursing major, but she wanted to work at a nursing home or assisted living center, so she focused her volunteering on those sorts of places. Not me. I wanted to be either an ER nurse or a nurse in the pediatric ward. I was using my volunteer time to figure out which one was a better fit.

"*Forever?*" I asked with a sideways look. I headed for the stairs, and Griselda followed.

"Well, fifteen minutes can seem like forever when you're freezing your tits off."

We weren't even to the second flight of stairs, and she was already breathless. The first semester we were roommates, she'd come to the gym with me a couple times before declaring that she intended to gain the freshman fifteen twice. She'd been joking, but that was when I'd seen how much it bothered her when people were rude about her being overweight. She didn't starve herself, but she ate healthy with the occasional splurge. Not that it was anyone's business but her own.

"Is there a particular reason you were waiting for me in your PJs even though it's four o'clock in the afternoon?" I asked. "Are you okay?"

"I'm wonderful." Her lips stretched into an overly wide smile. "I was going to spend the day lounging around, watching sappy holiday movies, but then something totally rad happened."

Every other day she found something 'totally rad' that she just *had* to tell me about. I was an only child, but I always imagined that having a sister would be a lot like how things were between Griselda and me.

"You're coming with me," she declared without any clarification.

"And where, exactly, am I going with you?"

"The Hamptons."

That stopped me before I could unlock the door to our apartment. "The Hamptons? Who do you know there?"

Griselda grinned, happy that she'd finally gotten my attention. She tossed her thick, raven-black hair over her shoulder. "Do you remember Doug, the guy I dated over the summer?"

"The lifeguard in Cabo?"

"That's the one." Her dark green eyes sparkled. "His parents, like, have this house in the Hamptons and they're letting him have a bonfire tonight."

"Weren't you just complaining that it was cold as hell?" I asked as I opened the door. "Why would you want to go somewhere outside?"

"Duh, that's, like, what the bonfire's for." Griselda plopped down on her bed and bounced a couple times.

"Besides, do you think I'd let a little thing like cold keep me from, like, scoping out totally smoking rich guys?"

"Sounds like your sort of party." I pulled off my scrubs and tossed them into my dirty clothes hamper. I needed to do laundry soon.

"It is," she said, still bouncing. "But, like, it's going to be your kind of party too. Tonight anyway."

I shook my head and wondered, not for the first time, if there was a way to get Griselda to stop using the word *like* in every other sentence. That was one particular fad I hoped died out fast. "I'm going to take a shower, put on something comfortable, and spend the rest of the day in bed reading."

"No," Griselda said firmly, crossing her arms over her chest. "You need to, like, get out more."

I rolled my eyes. "I get out plenty."

She rolled her eyes right back. "Out to something, like, other than class or volunteering at the hospital."

Okay, she had me there. I felt myself caving. "Will you be the only person there I'll know?"

I didn't mind parties or being social, but I wasn't fond of being the odd person out. I didn't know of anyone who did. But she was right that I hadn't been spending much time with people outside of work.

"I don't know," she said before bobbing her

eyebrows. "But I do have someone that you should get to know."

I narrowed my eyes at her. "Please tell me you aren't trying to set me up on *another* blind date."

"This one is a good guy, I promise."

"You said that about Patrick Charles," I reminded her, my face growing warm at the memory.

"How was I supposed to know that he was trying to make his girlfriend back home, like, jealous?"

I frowned at her. "You could have asked the same friend who interrupted dinner to tell Patrick that the girlfriend was on the way to dump him."

She had the grace to look at least a little bit embarrassed. "Okay, that was on me."

I pointed a finger at her. "And what about Timothy Bozer?"

"Hey, no one knew he was doing drag under the name Kitty Come Get Me. He was the head of the NYU Young Republicans!"

She looked so indignant that I had to laugh, but I still wasn't going to waste another night on one of her disaster dates.

"This guy's different," she insisted. "He's actually my cousin, so I know he comes from a good family. He's a couple years older than us, but not like creepy old."

"Gris–"

"Please, Abigail," she pleaded, her hands folded under her chin in a prayer. "I promise, if you come with me tonight and meet my cousin, I won't try to set you up with anyone ever again."

I snorted. "Yes, you will."

After a beat, she gave me a sheepish grin. "Yeah, I totally will. But not for a while."

An idea popped into my head. "I'll tell you what, I'll go tonight if you do my laundry and wash up the dishes while I get a shower."

She sighed. "All right. But you have to promise to stay for at least an hour."

"It's a deal," I said, rubbing my hands together. "Now, please let me get a shower. I'm tired of standing here in my bra and panties."

She laughed and waved me away. "I'll get out something for you to wear."

Something 'totally rad,' I was sure.

THREE
JAX HUNTER

December 22ND, Present Day

December 22ND, Present Day

Boston, Massachusetts

I couldn't even remember what I'd been doing a year ago today. Mid-January, I'd left Boston to go to New York City on business, and my entire life had changed forever. I'd followed a mysterious blonde into a place called Club Privé, and while at the BDSM club, I'd decided to open a similar place here in Boston. That decision led me to checking out various properties for the club site, which had taken me to a run-down bar owned by the feistiest brunette I'd ever met, Syll Reeve. Now, less than a year later, she was Syll Hunter, and I couldn't imagine my life without her.

So, yes, I remembered exactly where I'd been on January sixteenth, but had no idea what I'd been doing two days before Christmas Eve. This year, however, I had no doubt I'd remember everything.

"Mr. Hunter!" a tall, willowy red-head called out as she waved at me.

I went toward her, calling up her information in my head as I went. Justina Daniels, twenty-three, new bartender. I'd personally conducted the last interview after her background check had come back clean. She'd been overly excited about the prospect of participating in some of the more extreme aspects of *Pothos*, but she hadn't expressed any concerns with the rules I'd set out from the start when it came to that aspect of their employment here. Employees had strict guidelines about how, when, and with whom they could indulge in any BDSM or other sexual encounters.

"How's your shift going so far, Miss Daniels?" I asked once she was close enough to hear me without shouting.

"Great!" She beamed at me. "I've worked the whole week and every night is better than the last."

"I'm glad to hear it," I said as I resisted the urge to glance at my watch. I didn't want to be rude to her, but I did have somewhere I needed to be. "How can I help you?"

"I heard the club is going to be open on Christmas Eve and Christmas Day."

I searched for annoyance in her expression but didn't see any. "Yes, but I did the schedule differently. I promised time and a half for anyone who worked and then asked for volunteers, just like I did on Thanksgiving. If I hadn't received enough, we would have closed, but I was able to make a full schedule."

A lot of my employees had been surprised by my policy, but gratefully so. I remembered too many holidays where my grandfather had been too busy working to do more than put in an appearance, and after my grandmother was gone, he'd rarely even done that.

Syll, however, had been on the other end of things. Going two days without income had been rough on her. I paid well, but there were always extra bills to pay. We wanted to give our employees options.

"Are *you* going to be here?"

I managed to stifle both my sigh and my annoyance. Justina was hardly the first employee to try to charm me, and I doubted she'd be the last. Even after my looks went, I'd still have money, and there were plenty of women who cared more about that than anything else. Fortunately, my wife wasn't like that.

Which was one of the biggest reasons why she was my wife.

"Miss Daniels, let me make this clear so there is no misunderstanding. I am happily married and have no desire to be unfaithful to my wife, who, incidentally, is also the owner of *Pothos* and your employer."

Color flooded the young woman's cheeks, but I didn't let that stop me. She needed to hear everything laid out for her now, in no uncertain terms.

"As I mentioned in your final interview, all dating policies for employees are laid out in your handbook, as are the sorts of behaviors that result in disciplinary action. I will assume this conversation means you signed your contract without reading the section that states you will abide by all of the policies outlined in said handbook. Most employees do."

I gave her a few seconds to squirm. And squirm she did. "I'm–"

Holding up a hand to stop her from saying anything more, I plowed on, "Everyone receives one free pass for a minor infraction regarding those rules. This is yours. I suggest you thoroughly read your handbook and make a list of anything that's unclear so that it can be explained to you. If there are any policies that you feel are unfair or that you don't believe you can follow, you're welcome to quit at any time, though the NDA you signed will remain a legal and binding agreement, as stated in the contract you signed."

I rattled off everything with barely a pause and watched Justina's eyes grow bigger and bigger with every word. I'd given this speech a few times since the club's opening in October, but only one person had quit, and that one hadn't been a surprise.

That woman had flat-out told me that she couldn't follow the rule regarding the prohibition of extra-marital affairs in the workplace. If a married couple wanted to play, that was fine, but no way in hell would I let my club get caught up in a shitstorm if married employees decided to use work as a dating service. If an employee wanted to have an affair with someone outside the club, that was their own business. They just couldn't bring it in here.

"Oh, uh, I...I mean, that's not...shit." Face flaming almost as red as her hair, Justina spun around and hurried off, long legs wobbling on spikey heels.

"Boss, what are you still doing here?"

I turned toward Calvin Madden as he jogged up from his normal position at the door. He was the on-site manager tonight as well as the bouncer. He was a massive man, a former football player who'd retired after a third concussion had left him wondering if playing football was worth the risks. He'd actually been a member of security at Hunter Enterprises – the company my grandfather had more or less left to me – but when I'd asked if anyone was interested in moving to the club, Calvin had been the first volunteer.

Asking him to move to management had been a hunch on my part, but one that had paid off. Most people saw a big guy and immediately thought security, but I'd done my due diligence and found that he had a degree in office management. A conversation had revealed an interest in getting an MBA after his football career had ended, so we'd come to an agreement where he'd work in a management role while I paid for his degree, and in exchange, he'd be able to take over more of the day-to-day work at *Pothos* to allow my schedule to be freer. Once I made sure everything was on the right track.

"How long do you think it'll take for you to remember that you can call me Jax instead of Boss?" I asked with a genuine smile.

He grinned at me, white teeth flashing against dark skin. "A little while longer, Boss."

When his smile faded as quickly as it had appeared, I looked at him curiously. "Is something wrong?"

He lifted a broad shoulder. "Just wondering why you haven't left for your trip with that gorgeous wife of yours."

"I'm getting ready to leave right now," I said, then frowned at the reason for my delay. "Justina Daniels just needed a reminder of what is and what isn't appropriate at work."

Calvin grimaced. "I had a feeling that was the case. She's been overheard making comments about how attractive she finds you."

"Keep an extra eye on her while I'm gone," I said. "She might make a play for a couple of the other married guys. If she doesn't, great, but she's finished if she does. You can either take care of it yourself or let it sit until I get back."

"I'll take care of everything, Boss," he assured me. "Now, you'd better get going or Mrs. Boss is gonna be pissed she had to do all the packing herself."

I chuckled. "Yes, she will be."

"Have a safe trip."

"I will." I gave him a short wave as I finally made it out the door. If Calvin ended up taking the responsibility of firing Justina if necessary, I'd make sure he received an additional bonus when I returned.

Not for the first time, I wondered if it was a good idea for me to be leaving when things here were still so new. The club was doing extremely well, but I'd learned well under my grandfather. The first year was critical, and we weren't even to the first six months.

I'd already committed to these plans, though, and I'd have three annoyed brothers and one furious wife if I tried to back out now. I leaned back in my seat and closed my eyes, content to let my driver do his thing. I enjoyed driving, but I'd be getting my fill of it tomorrow.

About a month ago, I'd received a letter from my grandfather's estate regarding a cabin that none of us had known existed. It was in Hudson Valley, New York, about one hundred and sixty miles from here. Grandfather having something like that wasn't actually that far outside how he did things. It wasn't, however, under his name. It was under my grandmother's.

I'd done some investigating, but it hadn't been overly thorough, just enough to know that it was in good condition and big enough for my brothers, myself, and all of our wives. I couldn't remember which of us had suggested we use it over Christmas before we decided what to do about the cabin, but however it'd happened, my wife and I would be heading up there tomorrow morning to meet with my brothers and my sisters-in-law.

The trip would be good for Syll and me. It'd been a while since we'd been able to spend much time just the two of us. Well, it wouldn't only be us, but there wouldn't be any work to distract us, nothing stressful occupying our minds.

As we pulled up in front of the Hunter family home, I let myself hope that this would let us all end the year on a good note and give us something to shoot for in the coming new year.

FOUR
SYLL REEVE HUNTER

DECEMBER 23ᴿᴰ, PRESENT DAY

Hudson Valley, New York

With his expensively-cut sandy brown-hair and pale blue eyes, Jax Hunter looked every inch the classic Bostonian blue blood. All of the Hunter brothers were gorgeous – the sort of genes anyone would want in their family – but I wasn't remotely attracted to the other three. I'd only ever had eyes for Jax, even when I'd been furious at him. At the beginning, that had been more often than not.

The memories made me smile. It was hard to believe it had been less than a year since he'd shown up at my bar with an offer to buy it. I'd closed the door in his face that day, with no idea that I'd just met the person who'd change my life forever. At the time, I'd been dating a total asshole and trying to pretend that he just needed some polish.

"We should be there soon."

Jax's statement startled me. The car hadn't been completely silent, not with the Christmas music playing, but the only words Jax had said since we'd left Boston had been muttered curses at the worse-than-usual traffic to get out of the city. And that was saying something because, as much as I loved Boston, the traffic was horrendous.

"The roads don't look too bad." Even as I said it, I knew how inane it sounded.

"They're not."

And we were back to listening to Christmas music.

How had we gotten to this point?

We'd been married for only two and a half months and hadn't even been together for a year. Sure, things between us had escalated quickly, but he'd told me that he wanted to be with me forever. He'd wanted a partner.

Except I hadn't been feeling much like a partner recently.

When we'd opened *Pothos* in the place where my father's bar had once stood, I'd assumed I'd be working side-by-side with my husband, and for a while, it had been exactly like that. Through the planning and building, we'd often stayed up late or got up early, eager to make our dream a reality. I'd been on his arm for our entire opening weekend.

But then things changed.

Instead of being side by side with Jax, hands-on managing the club we both owned, he'd relegated me to the office. Administrative work. Making the schedules. Payroll. Ordering supplies. Ensuring the place was up to code and up to our standards.

My interactions with the staff I helped hire had been limited to the occasional greeting in the hall or if they came into the office for something specific. Clubs didn't run nine to five, but Jax wanted to have someone there during the day for deliveries and that sort of thing, so he had me working from eight until five, only there for an hour after the doors opened. Sometimes I stayed until six because that was when he came in, and if I left on time, I rarely saw him at home.

This wasn't the life I'd agreed to, but I didn't know how to tell Jax that without him thinking that *he* was my regret. I didn't want to lose him, and I certainly didn't want to hurt him. Just the thought of hurting him caused me pain, and I couldn't even think about him not being mine anymore.

"The cabin is one of the largest in the area," Jax said. "Four bedrooms, each with their own master bath, a half bath downstairs..."

I tuned him out as he gave me the same description that had come with the letter alerting us of the cabin's existence. I wasn't being rude. He'd said the exact same thing twice last night while we'd packed. It'd been pretty much the only thing he'd said.

Small talk.

Bullshit.

Where was the passionate man I'd verbally sparred with? The man I'd slapped shortly after our first kiss. The one whose voice could turn my insides to mush. The only man I'd ever let boss me around.

He was the man I wanted to have a family with, but that wasn't a discussion I felt like I could approach right now. Talking about starting a family soon should have been easy to do. Instead, I didn't know how to talk to him at all.

I'd done things with him that I'd never imagined, and I'd thought I could trust him with my life. I probably still could trust him with that, but I no longer knew if I could trust him with my heart.

"Here we are."

Jax's voice cut through my maudlin thoughts, and I scrambled to pull myself together. I couldn't let him see what was going on in my head, not now. The brothers had only just mended things between them. This was their first Christmas without their grandfather and with each other. I couldn't ruin that by bringing my concerns up to Jax, even if I did figure out how to express them.

"It looks like we're the first ones," I said with a smile. It didn't feel natural, but I was glad that I could manage something so simple.

"I'm sure the others will be here soon."

I couldn't tell if he was glad about that or not. The worst part was, I knew that a couple months ago, he would've loved for us to have time to ourselves here, if for no other reason than to bend me over the first piece of furniture we saw and take me hard and fast.

My pussy throbbed at the thought of having him inside me for the first time in weeks, and I almost suggested the whole 'bending me over the furniture' scenario myself. One look at the distracted expression on his face killed that idea though. While I was thinking about how much I missed us making love, he was probably running through inventory in his head.

"I'm glad they cleaned the stoop off," Jax said as he retrieved our suitcases from the trunk of the car. "I was assured that things would be spotless inside, but with last night's fresh snowfall, I wasn't sure they'd think to come up and clean off the outside."

I watched him walk toward the door, and instead of appreciating the way his ass looked in his jeans, I was struggling to keep back the tears burning my eyes. I wanted to talk to my husband. Really talk to him. Not listen to him yammer on about asinine shit like this.

Fortunately, a distraction arrived in the form of one of my new brothers-in-law and his girlfriend. From here, I couldn't tell which couple was in the gray Traverse, but I thought it might be Slade and Cheyenne since they were the only ones who needed room in their vehicle for someone besides the two of them, though not for this weekend. They didn't technically have any kids, but Cheyenne's little brother, Austin, had been raised by Cheyenne, and when Slade moved from Texas to Boston, he'd wanted them both to come with him. Now, the three of them were a family. Four, if I counted Estrada, another transplanted Texan who was practically Austin's godmother. A ready-made family.

As I plastered my fake smile on again, I wondered if I'd ever have any of that for myself.

FIVE

JAX

DECEMBER 23RD, PRESENT DAY

Hudson Valley, New York

I watched Blake throw another log into the fireplace and marveled at the fact that he was here. The youngest of us, he'd been the most distant over the years, dealing with the most guilt and grief over what had happened. He hadn't only lost his parents and sister. Aimee had been his twin, and I knew he imagined what she might be like had she survived the car crash.

The next two years were going to be hard for him. He'd turn thirty – the same age our mother had been when she died – and then thirty-one – our father's age when he died. Kids expected to outlive their parents, maybe even pass up the age they were when they died, but getting to that point when I wasn't even middle-aged had really thrown me.

"Don't think so hard, big brother. You'll give yourself wrinkles." Slade sat down next to me, baby blue eyes twinkling.

He looked the most like Mom except for his eyes. Those were Dad's, same as the rest of us. But we never talked about who we resembled. We had a lot of those subjects. Maybe now that we'd solved the mystery behind the car crash that had taken our parents and sister, we could share things without it hurting as bad.

Just not right now.

"How's Austin?" I asked. All of us had pretty much fallen in love with the kid from the moment Slade and Cheyenne had introduced us.

"Great." Slade beamed. "We had our own Christmas celebration with him yesterday, and he was so excited about getting to have another Christmas that he could barely sleep last night."

I glanced across the room where a petite young woman stood next to the eggnog, talking to Syll. Cheyenne Lamont and my brother didn't look at all like they belonged together. The artist and the former soldier.

Slade had joined the military right out of high school and had sported military-approved hair for years, even after he'd left the service and joined the DEA. Even now, with his hair long enough to be unruly, he had the clean-cut sort of appearance that screamed 'authority figure.'

His girl, on the other hand, barely looked over eighteen even though I knew she'd be twenty-two in a couple weeks. Her long platinum blonde hair had been streaked with pink just a couple months ago at my wedding, but now it was a deep blue that matched the cute velvet dress she wore. The lights flashed off her piercings, and I noticed that she'd cut down the number by about half.

"How's Cheyenne doing away from him?" I lowered my voice enough that only Slade could hear me.

"Better than we both thought, but it's still early."

Something tightened at the corners of his eyes, his mouth, and I wondered if it was from worry about Cheyenne over the next few days while apart from her brother, or if they were experiencing similar tension to what was between Syll and me.

As if he'd read my mind, Slade asked, "How are things with your lovely wife?"

I took a long drink of my eggnog, grateful that we'd brought both the alcoholic and non-alcoholic kinds. I wasn't a huge drinker, but I needed something to take the edge off while I tried to figure out how honest to be. If he'd asked me that question six months ago, I would've simply answered *fine* and let that be all. Now, however, we were at a place where we were all trying to repair our relationships with each other, and I didn't want to throw that away on a lie.

My gaze was drawn back to Syll and Cheyenne, but this time, my attention was on my wife. She was the same height as Cheyenne, but that was where the similarities ended. Syll had beautiful olive-green eyes that practically glowed when we made love. Thick cocoa-colored waves that were the perfect length for me to grab and pull when I took her from behind. Hips and an ass that were curved just right for my hands. Breasts and nipples...

Fuck.

A throbbing ache settled low in my stomach, and my cock thickened. It'd been too long since I'd been inside her. It hadn't felt right, asking her to be with me physically when we'd barely been together for more than a few hours a day since we'd returned from our honeymoon.

"We've been busy," I said honestly. "Trying to get *Pothos* off the ground takes a lot of time and energy."

"But you're not regretting marrying her?" Slade's question was sincere, curious rather than acrimonious.

"Not for a moment." I didn't even need to think about the answer. It might've taken me a while to admit that I loved her, but from that moment, I'd known that I wanted to spend the rest of my life with her.

I just hoped *she* wasn't regretting it.

Slade nodded and settled back in his seat, sipping his eggnog, a speculative expression on his face. I could've asked him what he was thinking, but Cai had just taken the seat on the other side of Slade and started up a conversation that had something to do with how much both the DEA and the CDC hated red tape.

"Since no one else is going to say it, I will." Blake's booming voice carried over everyone else's conversations.

He may have been the youngest, but he was the biggest at a muscular six feet four inches, and his voice made him seem larger than life. He and his fiancée, Brea Chaise, still lived in Wyoming, but he no longer looked like a gruff mountain man, something for which Brea was entirely responsible.

"How in the hell didn't we know about this place?"

"Blake, really?" Brea laid her hand on Blake's shoulder. She shook her head, raven-black curls bobbing. "We talked about this."

He flushed, and then reached up to put his hand over hers. A soft smile curved his lips, and despite everything I had going on in my own life, I took a moment to appreciate seeing it there. He'd rarely smiled after the crash and seeing him do it easily eased a tension I hadn't realized I was carrying.

"Sorry," he said. He captured Brea's hand and used it to pull her down onto his lap. She let out a surprised yelp that immediately turned into laughter. When he joined in, I wasn't the only person staring at them.

"There's a sound I never thought I'd hear," Slade said softly, his voice choked with emotion. Cai and I simply nodded in agreement.

"I'll behave myself," Blake said, kissing Brea's temple. He turned his attention to us. "Are you guys sure Grandma Olive never talked about owning a cabin? I was only eight when she..." He cleared his throat. "Maybe I don't remember it."

"I don't remember either of them talking about a cabin," Cai said. "Grandfather wasn't exactly the camping type."

"This isn't camping," Syll said with a laugh. "At least not any sort of camping I've ever done."

"When have the Hunters done anything normal?" Brea asked with a mischievous smile. "I mean, I haven't been a part of the family for long, but I'm pretty sure I have at least that MO right."

"She has a point," Addison said as she perched on the arm of the couch.

"Hey!" Cai gave Addison a surprised look. She

leaned over and whispered something in his ear that made his bright blue eyes go heated. "I'm going to hold you to that."

"Whether or not this could be called camping, I like it," Brea said. "I think maybe your grandma wanted this to be a surprise. One room down here. Four rooms for four boys upstairs. Boys that would have families one day."

"I wish she could have met you," Blake said.

I heard the sadness in his voice, but not the bitterness that had been present pretty much his whole life. Brea had been beyond good for him.

"She sounds like a lovely woman," Cheyenne said.

"She was," I replied. "Dad was a lot like her."

All eyes turned to me, each full of surprise. I understood why. I rarely talked about our parents, and pretty much never brought them up.

"If it's too painful, I understand," Syll said quietly, "but I know I'd love to hear more about him. About your mom too."

Pain went through my heart, but it wasn't as bright has it had been in the past, and I knew it was due to the people sitting here with me. I saw similar emotions flashing across my brothers' faces. I saw something else too. Hunger. A hunger to know more about our parents.

Sometimes, I forgot just how young we'd all been, how little Blake and even Cai probably remembered.

"What do you want to know?" I asked.

A soft smile curved Syll's lips as she asked, "How did your parents meet? Do you know?"

"I do." Judging by the way my brothers' eyes widened, I guessed they didn't know the story. I'd never thought to ask. A flash of guilt went through me. "One day when I was home sick from school, a year or so before the accident, Dad told me that they met at a party."

"A party? That seems so...trite," Addison said, clearly disappointed.

"Well," I took another drink, "there was a little more to it than that..."

SIX

CT

EVENING, DECEMBER 23*ᴿᴰ*, 1984

The Hamptons

If Finn didn't stop singing that obnoxious song, I was going to spend the new year in jail for punching my friend in the face. Then again, if I made a jury listen to "I Want a Hippopotamus for Christmas" for an hour straight, they'd probably give me a medal.

"Admit it," Finn said, his usual cheer in full force. "You're happy to be going out tonight instead of sitting back in your apartment, all by yourself."

I glared at him. "I was, until you insisted on singing that song."

"Then you need to sing with me," Finn said. "Pick a Christmas carol."

Dammit.

I knew Finn wouldn't give up until I agreed. I picked one of the least annoying ones that I knew, and then another. We'd made our way through pretty much every song I knew by the time we pulled up to one of the Hamptons massive houses. It had started to snow a while back, and the grounds were blanketed in thick, wet white. That hadn't prevented the driveway from already being packed with some of the most expensive cars I'd ever seen. Or the dozens of college-aged kids wandering around the property, apparently heading toward the massive bonfire on one side of the house.

I was only twenty, which meant I fit right in with this group age-wise, but as I got out of the car, I felt old. I'd been to a million parties like this back in Boston, bored rich kids pretending that they were better than others because they were at a party up here instead of a frat party in the city. Their beer was more expensive, their drugs premium quality. They bragged about the size of their trust funds and the cars they drove, but none of them had ever done a days' work in their lives.

That wasn't fair. With a crowd this size, at least a couple kids had probably had the occasional job. *I* did, after all, and my family's bank account could hold its own against most of the families represented here.

Not that I'd made that public knowledge. To my friends in New York, I was CT Hunter, wanna-be journalist. Hard worker who had his own place. Most assumed I came from a higher middle-class family, maybe a doctor or lawyer. Enough money that I wasn't scraping by, but that was it.

One of the reasons I'd wanted to come to NYU instead of an Ivy League school was also one of the top reasons I hadn't chosen to stay in my home state. In Boston, pretty much everyone knew me as Chester Thomas Hunter, only child and heir apparent to Hunter Enterprises. While people in New York might've heard of my family's company, I doubted they'd put two and two together, especially when I didn't use my given name.

A snowball hit the side of my neck, cold slush trickling underneath my collar. I whipped my head around to glare at Finn.

"What the hell?"

He grinned at me. "You're brooding."

I swiped the rest of the snow away. "I don't brood."

He raised an eyebrow. "Trust me, dude, you do."

I opened my mouth to argue, then snapped it shut. As much as it galled me to admit, he was right. I did brood. I might not be thrilled that he'd dragged me to a party – and an outdoor one at that – but that wasn't a good reason to be rude.

"What do you say we go grab something to drink?"

Finn slung his arm around my neck, our similar heights keeping me from needing to bend over to keep my balance.

"If all they have is that imported shit, you're going to owe me," I grumbled.

"Deal."

I felt eyes on us as we moved toward the bonfire, and I knew what everyone was thinking. Being Finn's friend and not freaking out when he did things like grab my arm had led to speculation that we were more than friends. When people asked, I told them the truth – that Finn and I were only friends – but other than that, I never felt the need to explain myself to the Neanderthals who thought that any man who was friends with homosexuals had to secretly be gay too. The attitude toward the gay community was getting better, but there was still a long way to go.

"My cousin's supposed to wait for us near the fire," Finn said. "She should be here already."

I nodded, but there was nothing enthusiastic in the gesture. I hoped she was here because I just wanted to get this over with.

Tables of food and drinks were set up a few feet away from the fire, the air and snow cold enough that ice wasn't needed. Chairs and benches were scattered around, and multi-colored lights twinkled from around numerous trees. The centerpiece of the whole thing was a massive bonfire. Easily three or four feet in diameter, logs built it up to at least six feet. Flames danced up into the indigo sky another two feet, sparks going even higher than that.

I was impressed despite myself. This was no slapped together party. Someone had either put a lot of effort into this or had hired someone to do the work. I leaned toward the latter, but it was still better than a bunch of drunken college kids huddled around a few tiny logs.

"Argus!" A female voice came from behind a group of people.

Finn dropped his arm, catching a tiny, dark-haired woman as she practically ran into him. He lifted her in a tight hug, then set her down and scowled at her. "What did I tell you about calling me Argus?"

She grinned, an impish look in her dark eyes. "I think you said I was the only one allowed to do it."

Finn rolled his eyes. "I'm pretty sure I did *not* say that, but you're not here to see me." He gestured to me. "Joy, this is CT. CT, my cousin, Joy Finn."

I held out a hand, and she shook it. "Nice to meet you."

"You too," she said. "I've heard a lot about you."

Finn reached out and put his hand on her shoulder. "I'm going to grab something to drink. Want anything?"

It was Joy's turn to roll her eyes. "Go away. Mingle. Flirt. Leave me and my date to get to know each other."

He put up his hands. "Fine, fine. I'll get out of your hair." He started to walk away, but then stopped and turned back to us. "Do you need a ride to Nana's tomorrow?"

"Bubby's coming to get me."

Finn flicked his fingers in salute and then headed off in the direction of the food.

"You and Finn are close?" I asked, sticking my hands in my jean pockets.

"We are. Our dads are twins, and Finn and I might as well be. We were born sixteen hours apart." Joy tugged off a glove and held out her hair to catch a few flakes. "I love snow."

"I usually do too," I said, watching the flakes land and melt. "But I like it clean like this, not dirty and slushy like it is in the city."

"You don't sound like you're from New York."

I let my slight accent thicken almost back to normal. "Boston, actually. Born and raised."

She grinned. "What brings you to the Big Apple?"

"School and the *New York Times*. I wanted to be a journalist at the *Times*, and I felt that NYU was my best chance at that."

She nodded as if it made complete sense to her.

"What about you?" I asked. "Finn's still got his nice Georgian drawl, but you sound more like you're from here."

"Close," Joy said. "We moved to New Jersey when I was twelve. I didn't like sticking out with my accent, so I learned to talk like my friends."

"First time I went back to Boston, everyone told me I talked like a Yankee now."

Back and forth it went, question and answer, first me then her. We went through likes and dislikes, areas of commonality and suggestions of new things to try. It was easy to talk to her, and surprisingly, we had a decent amount in common.

A graduate student at Brown, she was working on her master's degree in political science with plans of joining the Peace Corps and working in developing countries. Her entire face lit up as she talked about her plans, and I had no doubt that she'd be one of those people who actually followed through with everything. I admired that.

But it wasn't enough.

If I'd been looking for a friend, Joy would've been perfect. I wasn't one of those people who didn't believe that straight men and straight women could be only friends. My mom had taught me that.

One of the other pieces of relationship advice she'd

given me had been not to force something that wasn't there. And with Joy, that spark I was looking for wasn't there.

Sure, maybe an attraction could grow from friendship to something more. I'd seen it happen with friends of mine, both back home and here in New York. I supposed that could be possible with me, but I didn't think that was going to happen with Joy. She clearly had ideas for her life, a path set out, and so did I. Those paths, however, weren't going the same way.

"What about you?" Joy asked. "What are your plans for the future?"

My eyes met hers, and I saw the same truth written there that I felt. We didn't have a spark. I smiled at her and prepared to point out the elephant in the...yard.

But then, movement out of the corner of my eye caught my attention, and I turned my head.

Dark brown hair. Average height. Average build. Absolutely nothing that should have captured my attention.

My heart gave an unsteady thump. It was her.

SEVEN
ABIGAIL

Evening, December 23ʳᴰ, 1984

The Hamptons

I was going to kill Griselda. I'd put up with some crazy stuff from my roommate – the time she'd tried to smuggle a box of kittens into our room came to mind – but bringing me to a party in the Hamptons and then leaving me here with her cousin while she went off somewhere with an old ex, that was too far. I knew she didn't think things through, especially when it came to things that would never have bothered her had our positions been reversed, but she and I were going to have a talk about not abandoning friends at a party unless said friends were okay with it.

This friend was definitely *not* okay with it.

"Zelda says you're a nurse too." Theo Snowe finally

47

stopped talking about himself long enough to make a comment about me that wasn't *damn girl.*

"I am," I said politely. "So you call her Zelda? I'd never–"

"Yeah, that's what we called her when she was little." He made a strange sound that I supposed was a laugh. "Younger, since she never really was little. Am I right?"

I bristled immediately. "That's not exactly a nice way to talk about your cousin." I tried to come at it tactfully.

He shrugged his broad shoulders. "Yeah, well, if she doesn't like it, she should lose some weight."

I gritted my teeth and glared up at him. "Are you seriously defending making fun of your cousin for her weight and saying it's her fault?"

He shrugged again, and I was struck with the strong urge to do something drastic just to get a different reaction. Something like kicking him in the shins. Or the balls. Unfortunately, Griselda had vetoed my sturdy boots, and I was wearing a flimsy pair of dress shoes that were already soaked clear through. If I kicked him in these, I was more likely to break my toe than I was to hurt him.

"I have to admit, I was worried when she said she

had a friend she wanted me to meet. Zelda's friends in high school..." He shuddered. "Total dogs."

My jaw dropped. How in the world did Zelda not realize what an asshole her cousin was?

"But you," he paused to run his gaze over me from head to toe, "you're a smoking hot babe. A total fox."

"Thanks." I let sarcasm fill my voice, but he appeared clueless.

"I got my Thunderbird over there." He jerked his chin toward the long line of vehicles in the driveway. "Back seat's been nice and broken in. Wanna check it out?"

Before I could tell him exactly where he could stick his Thunderbird, something hard hit me from behind.

I flew forward, barely missing Theo and landing face-first in the snow. Everything was dark and wet as I struggled to get my hands underneath me. My lungs and throat burned as I swallowed snow, tried to breathe. A heavy weight was on my back, and I felt something hitting at my legs. I struggled, kicked, fought to turn over...

And then, suddenly, I was sitting up and coughing. My eyes stung as I tried to open them, but I did it anyway, blinking to clear the snow from my lashes. I kept coughing, gasping for air while only dimly aware of people talking around me. Then a face appeared in my vision. Golden blond hair that gleamed in the firelight and a pair of beautiful pale blue eyes. A strong jaw with some stubble.

Wow.

My stomach flipped.

Maybe my brain had been oxygen-deprived too long because I'd never had that kind of reaction to a guy before. Any guy. Ever.

"Are you okay?" He might've been asking the question for a while now, but it was only just now getting through.

"Dude, I said to get your damn hands off her!"

"I'm...confused." I thought for a second and then added, "And I'm wet."

"Sorry about that." He gave me the most charming smile I'd ever seen. "But I figured it was better to be wet than on fire."

I blinked. I must've still had snow in my ears.

"Dude!" Theo grabbed the blond man's arm and yanked him up. "Hands off my date!"

The stranger was leaner than Theo, but taller, and something about the way he carried himself told me that if my 'date' threw the first punch, the new guy would be the one left standing.

"Let go of me so I can help your date up, since you're apparently not going to do it." The stranger's tone was even, but there was no mistaking the warning.

Theo let go but glared at the man as he stretched out his hand to me. I took it, unable to stop staring at him. He gently pulled me to my feet, then wrapped his hand more securely around mine. The gesture could have come across as possessive, but to me, it merely felt protective. He'd let go if I pulled away. I knew it instinctively.

"Come on, Abigail," Theo said, holding out his hand. "We can still go check out my Thunderbird."

I stared at him, incredulous. "That's really your response to what just happened?"

"You're a real dick." The stranger said it so matter-of-factly that it took my befuddled brain a moment to realize that Theo had just been insulted.

"It's okay." I squeezed the new guy's hand and then let go, taking a step toward Theo. "I don't want to check out your car. In fact, no woman wants to be told that you've 'broken in' your car right before you try to get her to sleep with you. Not that I would've slept with you anyway. I have standards."

Color flooded Theo's face. "What did you say to me?"

It wasn't worth repeating so I just sighed heavily. "Just go away."

"You little–"

"You might want to think before you finish that sentence," the blond warned, taking a step closer to me.

The two men eyed each other for several long seconds as I held my breath. Then, sputtering incoherently, Theo stomped off, and I felt a sense of relief that he was gone. I turned back to the gorgeous guy with the golden hair.

"Mind telling me why you tackled me?"

"Sorry about that." The heat in his eyes belied the ease of his stance. "But you were on fire."

I blinked. "What?"

He reached out and unwound my scarf, not touching me as he did it, but the nearness was enough to make my skin tingle. I breathed slowly, taking in the sharp tang of smoke that seemed slightly different than it had a few minutes ago. It wasn't that or the scent of pine and snow, however, that had me mesmerized. It was him – either his cologne or his natural scent – and it distracted me enough that it took me a moment to realize that he was holding up the end of my scarf.

Or what used to be the end of my scarf.

It was burnt. Not just a couple spots where sparks had landed, but several inches had been reduced to nothing more than cinders.

"A gust of wind blew the end of your scarf into the fire. It caught the bottom of your coat too."

Startled, I looked down and saw that he was right. My coat had about half an inch of burned material along one side.

"I saw it from over there," he continued. "I tried yelling, but someone started playing that damn music."

I raised an eyebrow. "So your next idea was to tackle me?"

He scuffed his boot in the disturbed snow, the tips of his ears turning pink. "Yeah, I didn't really think that through. I was thinking more 'fire!'"

I laughed at his sheepish expression. A man as hot as him shouldn't be able to look adorable too. It wasn't fair. "I supposed I can look past it then."

He smiled, and I felt it all the way down to my soaking wet toes. "I'm CT, by the way."

"CT?"

He rubbed the back of his neck. "Chester. My real name is Chester Thomas Hunter, but I hate it, so I go by my first two initials. CT."

I held out my hand. "Abigail Slade. I just go by Abigail."

He shook my hand but didn't let it go. His fingers slid between mine, and I couldn't believe how natural it felt to hold on to him like this. How much I wished I wasn't wearing gloves. I wasn't one of those girls who came to parties to find a guy for the night. I didn't have anything against them, but it just wasn't me. I hadn't even been considering Theo's offer to check out his car. In fact, I'd been trying to figure out what I'd do if he did something like reach for my hand because the last thing I wanted was for him to touch me.

But I wanted CT to touch me. I wanted to hold his hand. I wanted more time with him. I couldn't explain it, this connection to a man I'd never even seen before tonight, but I couldn't deny it either.

A shiver ran through me from the soles of my feet to the top of my head. He tugged his hand free, frowning, but before I could wonder if I'd done something wrong, he had pulled off his coat.

"I'm such an idiot. You have to be freezing. We need to get you out of those wet clothes."

If he hadn't just then draped his coat around my shoulders and looked more concerned than horny, I might've been worried this whole thing had been a scam to get in my pants.

"Don't worry. I'm going to take care of you."

Somehow, I really believed he meant every word.

EIGHT

CAI

Evening, December 23ʳᵈ, Present Day
Hudson Valley, New York

"So, he told her not to worry, that he'd take care of her." Jax finished his story as the rest of us listened with rapt attention, captivated as much by the idea of something new as we were by his voice.

Syll leaned her head on his shoulder, and he tightened his arm around her, as if holding her had grounded him. When my big brother had told me that he'd fallen in love with the owner of the bar he was trying to buy, I hadn't known what to think. Jax was almost as logical and level-headed as me. While my field was science and his was business, the way we approached our work was similar. I hadn't been able to believe that he'd allowed emotions to cloud his judgment, and I'd sworn that would never happen to me.

Then I'd met Addison Kilar.

My eyes were immediately drawn to where she sat on the arm of the couch, next to me. Her brilliant orange-red curls were down, spilling over her shoulders in that wild way I loved. She was slender, almost delicate-looking, but stronger than she appeared. In fact, I frowned as I noticed that she'd lost weight. The skin beneath her pale green eyes was darker than the rest of her fair complexion even though I could tell she'd tried to cover it up. I'd known she wasn't sleeping well, but how had I missed the physical toll the last week had taken on her?

I reached over and took her hand, raising it to my lips. The surprise that lit up her face sent a flash of guilt through me. Like my brothers, my personality and my sexual preferences made me a Dominant, and I wasn't only one in the bedroom. We didn't go to the extremes that some couples chose, even in their day-to-day lives, but that awareness was always there between us.

She shouldn't have been surprised at the affectionate gesture.

Dammit!

Addison hadn't grown up in an abusive or neglectful home, but because of her high intelligence and independence, she'd often been left to her own devices. It was my responsibility to make sure she always knew how important she was to me, and I'd clearly failed in that department recently.

"I never knew our parents met while on blind dates with other people," Slade said, the light in his eyes dim.

I hated that Slade and Blake had so few memories of our parents and Aimee. Jax and I hadn't even been in double digits when they'd died, but Slade and Blake had only been five and four years old. Their memories were hazy at best and probably based as much on stories people told as they were on actual memory. Not that they'd even have much in the way of stories. As Jax's tale proved, we didn't talk about our parents often.

"There's a lot we don't know about them," Blake said, an edge of bitterness to his words. He'd been doing better, but I knew it'd take more than a few months to undo the damage that had been done to him. "No one really wanted to talk about them."

He said *we*, but none of us deluded ourselves into thinking that any of us had gotten the short end of the stick more than Blake. Our silence, and that of our grandparents, had done him a real disservice. More than that. It had left scars deeper than the rest of us had ever imagined.

"We're going to change that," Jax said. "It doesn't matter if it hurts to talk about them. We need to do it."

I could see my surprise reflected on my brothers' faces. To hear Jax talking like that wasn't something I ever expected. He wasn't the sentimental type. Or, at least, he hadn't been before he met Syll. The two of them were so good for each other, and they were going to make great parents to beautiful children.

"Excuse me," I said quietly as I pushed to my feet.

I didn't make eye contact as I made my way into the kitchen. It was small, but private, and that's what mattered to me. I needed a moment. If anyone noticed me leaving, they probably thought the talk of my parents was dredging up things I'd rather not remember, but that wasn't it at all. I actually liked the idea of getting to know more about the family I barely remembered.

It was thoughts of the family I didn't yet have that sent me from the room. Looking at my brothers with their women and realizing that they'd all have the chance to see themselves reflected in a child's face, it hurt more than I'd thought it would. I didn't begrudge any of them the children they'd have, whether soon like Blake and Brea, or later like the others, but that didn't make it any easier to see what I'd never have.

I served myself some more eggnog and lingered by the

punch bowl, not quite ready to go back yet. I hadn't had a lot of time to get used to the news that Addison's doctor had given us earlier this week, and I certainly hadn't had the time to process it. Everything had been focused on Addison and how she was handling the news. We were both doctors, though our fields weren't genetics or obstetrics, but understanding things on a logical, factual level was different than accepting what all of this meant for our actual lives.

How it changed everything.

I was supposed to care for her, protect her. It was literally my job to come up with answers and solutions to complex problems that could wipe out life on earth if things went badly enough. My IQ put me among some of the smartest people alive, and I'd never hurt for money or influence. There was nothing I wouldn't do for Addison, no line I wouldn't cross to give her all of the things that she deserved in this life.

The problem was, this wasn't something I could fix. Not with money or power or even with medicine. Sure, there were procedures that could possibly work around the medical issues, but they were dangerous, not to mention the low possibility of success. And that would be with only one attempt. Multiple births could happen, but if we wanted more than one child, it would raise the risk to Addison's life.

But if she wanted it, I would stand by her for every second, even if it killed me to do it.

I turned around and looked out the window, though I could see little outside. The moon was up, and what little I could see was bright. But as I watched, dark clouds passed over it often enough that I caught only glimpses of the trees around us. I'd always been more of a city person than an outdoor one like Blake, but I couldn't deny the beauty of this place.

I gratefully let thoughts of the mystery behind the cabin crowd out everything else. Those thoughts led to a number of questions tumbling through my mind.

Why had my grandmother purchased this cabin? Even more, why had she hidden it from us? Maybe she hadn't actually hidden it though. Maybe she'd just died before she'd had the chance to tell us about it. Or maybe she'd intended to present it to us at a specific time, like a gift.

I remembered the grief of each of my losses, but now the thoughts of them brought a new kind of sadness. Grandfather had been available for advice about things like school or business, but for something like this, he wouldn't have been any help. Well, if the issue had been money, he would've willingly helped with that, but when it came to the types of questions I wanted to ask, the sort of support I needed, he wouldn't have done me much good. I'd never missed Grandma Olive or my mother more than I had over the last few days, not even when I'd been pursuing Addison.

I closed my eyes, wondering if coming here had been a good idea after all.

A familiar touch made me open my eyes, and I didn't need to see her reflection to know that it was Addison standing behind me. The longer we were together, the more I felt as if I revolved around her, a planet to her sun. She was mine, the only person who'd ever managed to quiet the chaos in my head. The person who had become the most important person in the world almost from the first moment we'd literally run into each other. No matter what the future brought us, her place in my life wouldn't change. I needed her more than air, and I'd do whatever it took to keep her safe and happy.

NINE

ADDISON

Evening, December 23RD, Present Day

Hudson Valley, New York

Since meeting Cai, I'd asked him a few times about his parents and grandparents, but I'd never gotten much out of him. Knowing how young he'd been when they'd died, I'd assumed that he didn't remember much beyond his grandfather, but now I wasn't so sure. I didn't consider myself to be an overly demonstrative person, but in the short time I'd known the Hunter brothers, I'd learned that I was practically sappy by comparison.

When he'd left the living room, however, I suspected that it had more to do with our doctor's appointment this past Monday than it did with Jax's story. Having kids hadn't really been an 'if' issue with us, but more of a 'when,' and being the scientists we were, we'd both decided to have full work-ups so we would know of any issues before we officially started trying. Both of our families were dysfunctional enough that we knew there'd most likely be gaps in our medical histories, and we wanted to be as prepared as possible.

Except nothing had prepared me for the discovery that the chances of me getting pregnant were slim to none.

I wasn't a health nut, but I'd always taken care of myself. I barely even drank alcohol. But the reason I couldn't have children had nothing to do with the environment or my choices. Nothing I could've done differently, and no lifestyle change would alter the results. Understanding all of the medical terms didn't help. The fact of the matter was, biology had failed me.

When Cai didn't return after a few minutes, I excused myself and followed him into the kitchen. While things had only gotten to this point recently, the tension between the two of us had been there over the last few weeks. If I had to pinpoint a more accurate point of origin, Thanksgiving would have been the most logical choice. That had been the weekend we'd made the official decision to go for our medical work-ups.

It had also been the weekend my younger brother and his girlfriend had announced that they were pregnant.

The only thing that hurt worse than learning that I'd most likely never become pregnant was finding out that Gene had accidentally gotten Sandra pregnant despite the fact that they'd been using birth control. And they didn't want a baby.

Cai was standing at the counter and didn't acknowledge my presence as I entered the room behind him. I took a moment to appreciate the beautiful man who'd claimed me as his own. Golden blond hair, bright blue eyes, and the body of a god. At almost six and a half feet tall, with the build of an athlete, my thirty-two-year-old boyfriend could hold his own against athletes ten years younger.

As a total science nerd for as long as I could remember, I'd been crushing on Dr. Cai Hunter since I was a teenager, but I'd only recently learned that he'd also been an athlete in high school, receiving scholarship offers from numerous colleges to play basketball or run track. He'd turned them all down. Instead, he chosen to go to the University of California to study medicine.

I suspected its location had held a lot of appeal. Until their grandfather had used his will to essentially force the brothers into making amends, they'd all lived in different states and rarely spoke. Now, things could sometimes still be awkward, but all of us women agreed that the guys wanted to be involved in each other's lives, and we'd bend over backward to make sure that continued.

I closed the distance between us and slid my arms around him, clasping my hands an inch or two above his bellybutton. Closing my eyes, I rested my cheek on his back, drawing strength from his touch.

I'd always tried to pretend that I didn't need anyone else, that I was strong enough to do everything myself, and I supposed it would've been possible. I was thankful, however, that I'd learned the sort of strength it took to let someone else be in control for a while. When I was with him, touching him, the never-ending commentary that ran through my brain from the time I got up until I finally fell asleep stopped. He was the only person who could give me the peace of a blank mind.

I drew in a deep breath, taking comfort in the familiar scents of him. Of home. Even here, with the rich smell of cinnamon and eggnog permeating the air, I could make out the Irish Spring soap he used and the fabric softener I'd bought a couple weeks ago, converting him from dryer sheets to that sickeningly adorable bear.

He'd made a joke about it when he'd seen the bottle, teasing that no kid of his was going to snuggle with that damn bear. We'd shared a laugh over it on Thanksgiving too, just before Gene and Sandra had made their announcement and completely destroyed any of the day's levity.

Their announcement hadn't only been about an unplanned pregnancy. If that had been the case, my family would've rallied behind them, no matter how shocked or skeptical we were on the inside. No, it had been their plans that had derailed everything. Plans that involved giving their baby up for adoption.

I'd known that Sandra's family was highly religious. Her parents had been furious when she and Gene had moved in together without getting married. I doubted a baby born into that 'situation' would have made things any better. But they were also against abortion, so terminating the pregnancy was out.

I didn't know Sandra well, but I'd gotten the impression that the only two choices her family would have been satisfied with would have been a wedding or an adoption. Sandra could have defied them and gotten an abortion anyway, but I suspected she'd spent too many years with her family constantly talking against it to be able to make that decision without a lifetime of unbearable guilt.

I loved my brother, and I got along with Sandra well enough, but I was glad they weren't going to keep the baby and try to raise it on their own. Gene was twenty-one and had been working in furnace and air conditioning repair since high school. The guy who'd taken him on as an apprentice didn't have any kids, so Gene was being groomed to take over. Sandra was two years younger than Gene and had been taking online classes to earn a degree in office management. They didn't have a lot of expendable income, but they were definitely on their way to a comfortable life. Putting their baby up for adoption would protect their future plans and keep them from ever resenting the child for his or her own unplanned birth.

I was just thankful that they were being smart about it and thinking of what was best not only for them but for the baby too.

More than that, an idea had been growing inside me from the moment Gene and Sandra had dropped their bomb at Thanksgiving dinner. An idea that would ensure my brother and his girlfriend wouldn't have to cut off all ties to their child. That my family could still know the little boy or girl. An idea that could possibly fix the problem between Cai and me.

I wanted us to adopt the baby.

I hadn't talked to Gene or Sandra about it, but I was confident they'd agree. Since we lived far enough away, it wouldn't be too difficult to keep from confusing the child. And it would give Cai and me a family that didn't require a lot of medical procedures.

All I needed now was to figure out how to approach the idea without sounding like I'd either been scheming behind his back or was being too impulsive.

As much as I loved this idea, I couldn't help but wonder if Cai would want to adopt, let alone adopt from a family member. I wanted to look into my baby's eyes and see a hint of me, but I would be content to see similarities in things other than physical characteristics. And with Gene being my brother, there was always a chance the baby would look like me anyway. Cai wouldn't have that bond, and I didn't know how important it was to him to be able to see himself in our child.

I sighed. Far too many variables and unknowns. I just wanted to curl up in Cai's arms and let him take care of everything. I didn't want to deal with this anymore.

TEN
CAI

EVENING, DECEMBER 23RD, PRESENT DAY

Hudson Valley, New York

I felt Addison sigh more than I heard her, and my heart twisted painfully. I hated that there wasn't anything I could do to help her.

Well, almost nothing, because I could – and would – support her. I'd do whatever needed to be done on my end, and then be by her side for every moment of every medical procedure. At least we lived in a time and place where we had medical options. We didn't know if any of them would work, but I'd use every resource at my disposal, and even go to my brothers if necessary. I wouldn't give up, no matter how terrified I was of Addison enduring all of those tests and procedures. This wasn't about me. It was about her.

It was always about her.

I wrapped my fingers around her slender wrists and pulled her around until she was between me and the counter. I put her arms behind her back, bringing her body closer until she was leaning against me. She relaxed into me, and I closed my eyes, breathed in the scent of her. When I kissed the top of her head, she shivered, then tipped her head back, hunger and need stark on her face. Blood rushed south.

"What are you wearing under that skirt?" I asked quietly, keeping my grip on her wrists.

Her pale green eyes darkened. "The red satin panties you gave me for Jax and Syll's wedding."

My stomach clenched. "I like those, Little Red."

She smiled. "I know...Sir."

Damn, I loved it when she called me that. It reminded me of our first time together, that night at the club when neither of us had known who the other was. I'd been her first, and it hadn't taken me long to know that I wanted to be her only. That I wanted her to be my only for the rest of our lives.

I hadn't actually proposed to her yet, but that was because I wasn't exactly sure how she felt about marriage in general. We'd been talking about kids, and I knew that, for both of us, that meant a lasting commitment, no matter what it was called.

Except now, children might not be possible, and I didn't know if that changed things for our future.

"Take off your panties," I said, my voice rough. I needed her...*now*.

"I need my hands to do that."

I released her wrists, and a moment later, those red satin panties were hooked on her finger. I pocketed them as I leaned down to take her mouth. Cinnamon and nutmeg, the smooth taste of the expensive rum we'd brought exclusively for the eggnog, all of it coated my tongue, mingling with the taste of her. If anyone ever asked me what my favorite flavor was, I'd have to say Addison. Whether it was her mouth, pussy, ass, skin, it didn't matter. I just loved the taste of her.

"What should I do to you right now, Little Red?" I murmured against her mouth. My teeth scraped her bottom lip, nibbled at it. "My brothers and their women are only a few feet away, but I don't want to wait until we're in our room. I need to see you come now. Here."

Another shiver went through her, and I had no doubt that if I put my hand between her legs, I'd find her wet. I'd never share her, and my brothers would never consider asking any more than I'd ask them for Syll, Cheyenne, or Brea. That didn't mean the excitement that came with a semi-public encounter was any less.

"Tell me, Little Red," I continued. "Should I slide

my fingers inside you right here, finger you to orgasm so that every time you come into the kitchen over the next few days, you'll think of my fingers in that hot, wet pussy?"

Her tongue darted out to wet her kiss-swollen lips.

"Or should I take your ass? Bend you over the counter right here and push my way inside? Force you to keep quiet."

She whimpered, and my cock twitched. Damn, I loved when she made that sound.

"Unfortunately, I don't think we have enough time for the latter, and the first isn't going to do me any good, is it?"

She shook her head, those wild curls of hers tempting me. One of my favorite things to do was bury my hands in that soft fire, whether it was to pull her hair when I took her from behind or to control her movements when she went down on me.

I didn't have to ask her if she remembered her safe word even though she'd never used it. She would if she felt like she needed to, but in our relationship, being a good Dom meant keeping her from ever needing it. I also didn't have to ask if we had any condoms since we hadn't been using them since only a couple weeks after we started sleeping together. All of that meant that it was a simple thing for me to take her hand and pull her into the small alcove that currently held our boots and coats.

Her hands scrambled between us, tugging down my zipper even as I shoved her back against the wall. My eyes locked with hers, and I grabbed her thigh, lifting her leg to hook around my waist.

I let her feel the tip of me brush against her core, and then I entered her with one deep thrust. Air rushed out of her, and she grabbed my shoulders, nails biting even through my shirt. I reveled in the faint pain. I wasn't a sadist or a masochist, but I did appreciate the edge that certain types of pain gave pleasure, and I'd found that Addison shared that appreciation. For me, it was her nails, and for her, my teeth. We didn't always take things far enough to leave bruises or scratches, but we both enjoyed the occasional marks of ownership.

She moaned, and I clamped my hand over her mouth, making a chiding sound even as I put my lips at her ear. "Shh, Little Red. You need to come quietly. Think you can do that?"

She shook her head, little cries muffled against my palm as I drove into her with hard, bruising strokes. We didn't have much time, not if we didn't want someone to come looking for us, but I knew how to get us both off quickly. Taking our time was something we both enjoyed doing, but there was something to be said for the power of a fast, near-brutal orgasm.

I released my grip on her leg and buried my hand in her hair, yanking her head to one side. I buried my face against her neck, squeezing my eyes closed as I pushed away thoughts of red-haired children and the future that might never be. For the next few days, we'd live in the moment, talk about the past, but leave the future for conversations held at home.

Her body stiffened, back arching. I felt her scream more than heard it, but I would've known she was climaxing anyway by the way her muscles tightened around me. Each spasm that went through her body pushed me closer to the edge until I bit down on her neck to stifle my own cries of pleasure as I emptied myself inside her.

Even as I came, I felt a stab of sorrow at the knowledge that what we'd done, the love we shared, would probably never result in the creation of a child. Even if we went through all of the medical procedures and Addison did get pregnant, this wouldn't be the way it would happen.

I held her for a long minute, breathing in the scent of her, loving the feel of her. As much as I wanted the physical sensations, I also needed the time to compose myself. I couldn't let her know how scared I was that, in our quest to have a child, I'd lose her. I would be the rock she needed for as long as she needed.

By the time we made it back into the living room, I was pretty sure everyone knew what we'd been doing, but we'd both cleaned up, and I felt more in control of... well, of right now.

"Do any of you have any other stories about Mom and Dad dating?" Slade asked as Addison and I returned to our seats.

"Actually, I do." My brothers gave me a surprised look. "I overheard Mom talking one time about what happened the night they first met. I didn't know about the party in the Hamptons, but I guess this must've happened when Dad was taking her home. It started to snow..."

ELEVEN
CT

Night, December 23rd, 1984

The Hamptons

The snow was coming down harder now, and the party was slowly moving inside. I'd been standing next to Abigail at the fire for several minutes, trying to understand what it was about her that had instantly mesmerized me, when I realized she was still shivering. I offered her my coat and suggested we find a way to get her out of her wet clothes, but she refused, saying that the fire would dry her off fast enough.

I wasn't sure if she felt like she needed to prove that what had happened hadn't shaken her or if she didn't trust me enough to take care of her like I'd promised I would, but until I knew she was safe at home – wherever that might be – I refused to leave her side. That asshole date of hers had stormed off, but he'd struck me as the sort of guy who'd come back when she was alone to take revenge in some form. I had no doubt Abigail Slade was a fighter, but that didn't mean I'd let that dick near her as long as she was with me.

"Do you live around here?" I finally asked, needing both to break the silence and to know more about her.

She gave me a wary sideways glance. "Do I look like I'd have a house in the Hamptons?"

I gave her my most charming smile, gratified to see a flash of amusement in her dark eyes. "You don't *not* look like you belong here."

She turned, angling her body more toward me than the fire. I'd never wanted anything more than I wanted to get a better look at her...except to simply know her better. Being a journalist meant I had a natural curiosity and succeeding in my field required a tenacity that I had as well. Once I focused on something – or someone – I didn't let up until I got what I wanted. And I wanted her. Unless she made it clear that she didn't want anything to do with me, I planned to pursue her.

The decision came as a revelation to me, something I hadn't expected when I'd tackled her to the ground to put out the fire, but as soon as I put my thoughts into specific words, they made perfect sense. I considered myself a logical person, not prone to flights of fancy, but

I didn't have any real explanation for the way I was drawn to this stranger.

"I'm a student at NYU," she said, finally answering my question. "What about you? Are you a Hamptons' man?" A smile played around her lips.

I couldn't tell her that my family had one of the biggest houses around here, not when I could see it written all over her face how much she disliked it here. Besides, it wasn't as if I actually *liked* the whole Hamptons vibe. Even when I'd still been living at home, and I'd been forced to come here with my parents, I'd never been like the rest of the kids. My parents were rich. I wasn't.

"I went to NYU too," I said, "but I graduated. I work for the *Times* now."

One eyebrow arched rather quickly. "You're a reporter?"

"I am." A strange feeling of pride filled me at the impressed look on her face. I wasn't used to people reacting positively when I told them what I did. Probably because my parents had been furious when they'd realized I wasn't going to follow in my father's footsteps.

"Not what I imagined you'd be doing for a living," she said.

"What did you think I was going to say?"

"Firefighter, of course."

I had to force out a laugh, not because it wasn't funny but because her smile lit up her entire face and it took my breath away. Then she shivered, and I realized her teeth were chattering, and it stopped being funny.

"It looks like the snow's sending everyone inside. Do you want to go in?" I gestured toward the house. The bonfire was already fading, and only a handful of people were still outside, most of whom were pretty plastered.

Abigail shook her head, but she wrapped her arms around herself, tucking her hands under her elbows. "I only came tonight because my roommate is insane and wanted to set me up with her cousin."

I wanted to offer her my coat again but knew she would refuse. "The dick with the Thunderbird?"

She laughed, but the sound was broken up by her teeth clicking together, and that was more than I could take. I stepped closer and put my hands on her arms, rubbing up and down in the hopes that the friction would give her at least a little heat until I could convince her to let me get her someplace warmer.

"And that's why I now hate my roommate."

I laughed this time. "The guy over there talking to a tree is my friend Finn. He set me up tonight too, and there's a good chance that I'm going to steal his car and strand him here."

"You didn't like the girl he set you up with?"

I shook my head, keeping my voice light. "Someone else caught my attention."

She shrugged, a smile playing on her lips. "Sometimes you have to light yourself on fire to get out of awkward situations."

"I'll keep that in mind."

"CT! There you are!" Finn draped his arm around my neck. "I've been talking to that big galoot over there for five minutes, thinking it was you."

"I'm pretty sure that's a pine tree, Finn."

My friend frowned at me, and then looked back at the tree. "Is it?"

"I don't think you should drive tonight," I said.

"That's a good idea." His words slurred together, but he at least seemed like he was in a good mood. His bleary gaze shifted to Abigail, and he squinted at her. "You're not my cousin."

"No, Finn, she's not. This is Abigail. Your cousin went into the house about twenty minutes ago with a future Republican Senator."

"Damn her," Finn declared loudly with an off balanced stomp of his foot. "We don't need more of those in the family."

Abigail made a noise, and a quick glance told me she was trying to hold back her laughter.

I couldn't stop from smiling too. "You know what,

Finn," I said in my most reasonable voice, "why don't I take you to the house to find her? She can give you a ride home, right?"

He frowned, trying to sort things out in his drunken mind. "Are you trying to get rid of me?"

"Yes," I answered truthfully and held out my hand. "Give me your car keys."

"Why should I do that?"

"Because you're drunk," I said, hand still out. "And I need to take Abigail back to NYU."

He cackled. "You want to have sex with her."

Color rushed into Abigail's cheeks, and I smacked Finn on the back of the head. "Behave yourself."

"It's okay," he stage-whispered to Abigail. "I don't want to have sex with you. I'm gay."

"Okay, that's it. You're going inside." I put my arm around his waist to get him more upright, and then I glanced at Abigail with an apologetic look. "His keys are in his coat pocket, and the car is over there. It's the one with the Harvey Milk bumper sticker. Get in, start it, get the heat going. I'll be right there."

As I headed for the house, I didn't let myself think too long about the possibility that Abigail would simply take Finn's car and go on her own. She didn't really seem like the sort to steal a car, but maybe she wouldn't look at it as stealing if she left it for Finn somewhere. I hoped she did as I said though. Aside from the fact that I wanted to spend the drive to NYU learning more about her, I had a bad feeling that the weather was going to get worse, and I didn't know how comfortable she was driving, let alone on snow. A lot of people who lived in New York didn't drive.

"I think you like that girl," Finn said. "She likes you too."

"Really?" I asked, amused. "Not ten minutes ago, you were talking to a tree."

"That is a good point," he conceded. "I really did think you and Joy would get along."

"She was nice," I admitted, "but that spark wasn't there. We both knew it."

"But you have a spark with Abby back there."

"I do." I managed to open the front door without dumping my friend on the front step. The party hadn't missed a beat, and no one even batted an eye when I deposited Finn on the couch. "Are you sober enough to remember to find Joy?"

He shrugged. "If not, I'll sleep here and figure out a ride in the morning." He waved his hand dismissively. "Take care of your girl."

I didn't explain to him that Abigail wasn't my girl, but I was determined to find out if she could be. The sooner, the better. The thought moved me forward, hustling back to the last place I'd seen the pretty brunette, hoping the entire time that she hadn't taken off on me. If she had, I wouldn't have any choice but to go to NYU and talk to every student until I found her. I was a reporter. I could do that.

But I was really hoping I wouldn't have to.

She wasn't by the bonfire, but I could see Finn's car was on and still parked in the same place. By the time I got there, I was chilled clean through, but my heart was racing, and I barely noticed the cold. I got into the driver's seat and brushed the snow from my shoulders, giving Abigail a tight smile. Now that I was in the car with her, I found my tongue tied.

"Thank you for taking me home." She broke the silence for me. "I don't know where Griselda went and I'm pretty sure I'm not speaking to her for a while after that disaster of a date."

"Was it really a complete disaster?" I asked as I maneuvered the car around to head back down the driveway. "It brought us together, after all."

"True," she said. "But I think the fire had more to do with that than Griselda's horrible cousin."

"But neither of us would've been here tonight if it wasn't for our meddling friends."

"Also true," she agreed. After a beat, she added,

"Thank you, by the way. I realized that I'd been too shocked to say that before."

"Anyone else would've done the same."

"But no one else could have tackled me quite so well."

I laughed, but the sound was strained. Not because of what she said, but because the roads were worse than I'd imagined. It was still snowing, the glare of the headlights turning the world around us into the sort of brilliant white that would've been beautiful if it hadn't been dangerous.

"It wasn't this bad when we came in."

"No, it wasn't."

She'd managed to find some music that wasn't annoying while I'd dropped off Finn, and for a while, it was the only sound in the car. It wasn't an uncomfortable silence because I knew we could've found dozens of things to talk about if I hadn't been worrying so much about the way the tires were sliding on the ice and snow.

And then, suddenly, we were sliding too.

I fought with the wheel as the brakes locked and we spun around. Abigail grabbed my arm, a surprised sound that was somewhere between a scream and a shout. Then, we stopped as suddenly as we'd started, the rear end of the car slamming into something at a tilt.

"Are...are you okay?" I managed to ask after taking a couple deep breaths.

"I am," she answered breathlessly, her hand still tight on my arm. "You?"

"Yeah." I nodded as I looked around. "I think we're in a ditch."

Abigail's laugh had a slightly hysterical edge to it, and I wondered if she'd let me make this up to her or if I'd completely ruined everything.

I heard the click of her unbuckling her seatbelt and looked over in time to see her lean toward me...and then her mouth was on mine.

TWELVE
ABIGAIL

Night, December 23RD*, 1984*

The Hamptons

I could be a little spontaneous, but I'd never considered myself impulsive until the moment I kissed CT Hunter.

I'd been thinking about it almost non-stop since I'd been able to wrap my brain around the whole 'tackled because I was on fire' thing. The whole time while I was standing by the bonfire, pretending that I cared about the weather, I was wondering what it would feel like to be kissed by a man like CT. I'd been kissed before, but not anything memorable, not like how I knew it would be to kiss this particular man.

Then we ditched the car, and I decided that I didn't want to wait for him to make the first move. I felt his surprise for only a second before he responded, his hands going to my hair, fingers digging in as his mouth moved with mine. His lips were warm and much softer than I'd imagined. He leaned into me, then stopped, jerked back by his seatbelt.

He broke the kiss with a breathless chuckle and took a minute, resting his forehead on mine. Air rasped in and out of my lungs, the sound loud inside the mostly quiet car. The snow had already covered the windshield, and every glass surface was fogged over, creating a cocoon-like atmosphere where it seemed like we were the only two people in existence. My whole life, I'd never been as aware of another person as I was of him right then.

"Well, that was...unexpected." His fingertips traced lightning down my cheeks. "Unexpected, but not unwelcome."

I smiled, relieved that whatever this was between us, it wasn't one-sided.

I'd been on the occasional date, but nothing had ever gone beyond a kiss or two, and I'd never initiated any of them. It wasn't like I'd been saving myself for someone, but I wasn't about to give myself a second-rate first time simply because of some notion that the only way to take control of my sexuality was to have sex with multiple people as soon as I was 'ready' at fifteen or sixteen.

"I was worried it was all me," he said. His thumb

moved lazily along my bottom lip. "I've never felt like this before."

"Me either," I confessed.

He curled his fingers around the back of my neck, his eyes locked with mine. He was going to kiss me, and I knew if I allowed it, whatever was happening between us would become something more. I didn't know how long we'd be stuck in this car, and that meant I didn't know how far we would go. I didn't know how far I *wanted* to go...

I made a small, blissful sound the moment his lips brushed against mine, and I realized that I was thinking far too much.

He pulled me over the console between us, skillfully maneuvering me until I straddled his lap. I wasn't aware he'd removed his seatbelt until I no longer felt it between us, but it seemed like the least of things I needed to concentrate on. He pressed a hand against the small of my back, holding me tight against him even as his tongue swept between my lips. I wrapped my arms around his neck, letting him explore my mouth.

The car was still running, but all of the heat was generating between us. He pushed his jacket off my shoulders and tossed it into the seat next to us. My coat followed it, leaving me in my thin, fitted sweater, but even that felt like too much. I wanted to crawl out of my skin. Crawl under his skin. I wanted to be closer to him, feel him...

His teeth scraped over my bottom lip, and I moaned, an embarrassing sound that brought heat to my cheeks. I squirmed on his lap and was gratified to hear him make a similar noise. I gripped the shoulders of his shirt, pulled at it. He laughed, breaking the kiss to pull his shirt over his head. He tossed it up onto the heating vents.

"Might as well let it dry a bit."

I heard him, but all of my attention was on the fine specimen of manhood in front of me. I was pretty sure that I'd never uttered the words *fine specimen of manhood* before, but if they could ever be applied to anyone, it was this man right here. A beautiful lean body with cut, defined muscles over every inch I could see.

And ink.

"What's this?" I asked, running my finger over the design.

"An olive branch." His voice was shaky. "For my mom. That's her name."

I leaned forward and pressed my lips to the tattoo. He sucked in a breath, fingers tangling in my still-damp hair.

"I like it. Much better than a typical 'mother' tattoo."

He took my mouth in another toe-curling kiss, tugging me closer until the heat from his body seeped through my shirt to my hardening nipples. I let my hands roam over soft skin and hard muscles, greedily taking in every dip and curve. His free fingers slipped under the hem of my sweater, drawing patterns on my skin that made every inch of me tingle.

How had I never known that it could be like this?

Or maybe I'd known all along and that was why I'd been waiting. I'd wanted someone who could make me feel like this.

When his hands slid around my waist and moved up my ribcage, I knew where he was going. He'd stop if I asked him to, I had no doubt about that. He wasn't like Theo. Which was why I didn't want CT to stop.

"Please," I whispered. "I want you to touch me."

He bit down on my bottom lip again. "You don't think this is too fast?"

He had a point, but I didn't care. "No sex...but I want your hands on me."

CT nodded but didn't instantly grab me the way I'd thought he would. I could feel the strength and power in him, feel how much he held himself in check. When his hands finally moved up and around enough to cup my breasts through my bra, a shiver went through me, and it had nothing to do with the temperature outside. His thumbs moved over my nipples, chafing the sensitive skin with friction and soft cotton.

"You're gorgeous, you know that?" He pressed a kiss to my jaw, and then to my collarbone. "But I don't believe for one moment that's all you are. I want you, but I want all of you."

Despite our current situation, I didn't think he was only talking about sex. And neither was I when I responded, "I want all of you too."

He raised his head, his expression serious. "This should be crazy, right? Us feeling like this so fast?"

"It should be," I agreed. "But it's not, is it?"

"No," he said. "I can't explain it, but there's something between us. Something I don't want to ignore."

"Me either."

"Then this doesn't end when we get pulled out of this ditch." It wasn't phrased as a question, but I didn't need it to be. "What are you doing tomorrow?"

This was a strange conversation to be having. "Working in the morning and early afternoon, but after that, nothing. I wanted to work as much as I could at the hospital over break, so I told my parents I was staying at school."

He smiled and twisted some of my hair around his finger. "Would you come to a Christmas Eve party my parents are having here tomorrow evening?"

"You want me to meet your parents?" I probably

should have been freaking out, but I was still in the stunned phase.

He brushed his lips across mine. "I want you to meet everyone, and then I want to spend the holiday with you. The first of what I hope will be many."

When I'd left my room with Griselda earlier today, this was not how I'd expected the night to end, but it was better than anything I could've hoped for. Of course, there was only one thing I could say.

"Yes."

THIRTEEN
SLADE

N IGHT, *D*ECEMBER 2 3*ᴿᴰ*, *P*RESENT *D*AY
Hudson Valley, New York

"Mom accepted the invitation, and an hour or so later, someone driving by happened to see the car and used their truck to get them out of the ditch, get them back on the road."

Cai finished up his story in the same matter-of-fact tone that he'd used to tell the rest of it. He wasn't much of a storyteller, but he didn't have to be to keep us all entranced. It was a story about our parents we'd never heard before. For Blake and me, both had been new.

For several minutes, the only sound in the room was the crackling of the fire. No one moved or spoke, and I knew we were all trying to absorb the many emotions these stories had brought up.

A part of me that I hadn't known about before was aching now. Each of the four of us had found our own roles to play after the accident. Jax had become Grandfather's surrogate son and our surrogate father. Cai had hidden himself in books and tests, the ardent and accomplished student who became the brilliant doctor and scientist. Blake had been the angry one, the only one of us who'd shown genuine emotion, and the one we'd all felt the need to protect. He'd eventually turned into a recluse, only recently brought out of his shell by Brea.

I'd been the funny one. According to Jax and Cai, I'd been that way before, but I remembered making a conscious decision not long after we'd moved in with our grandparents. I would be the one to make everyone smile again. It became my shield, my way of deflecting more than dealing. I'd never let myself miss my parents or sister, and now I felt their absence in a way I'd never imagined.

The clock on the mantle chimed, breaking the silence. We blinked, shook ourselves as we came back from wherever our thoughts had taken us. Before things could get awkward, Cheyenne stood.

"I really should call Austin to tell him good night," she explained. "He'll never get to sleep if I don't."

I pushed myself to my feet, feeling almost drunk as I waited to see if my legs would hold me. I hadn't had enough of the eggnog to even be tipsy, but I already knew that wasn't what had me wobbly. This whole day had been strange. No, if I was being completely honest, the last few weeks had been strange. The past couple hours had only been the most recent of it all.

"I want to say good night too."

As if my declaration had granted permission to everyone else, the other couples quietly excused themselves as well, and we all made our way upstairs, no one speaking even as we moved into our individual rooms. The mood that had settled on us tonight was a somber one, and I couldn't help but wonder if the others were having private tensions as well.

"He'll probably want me to read him a story over the phone," Chey said, "which means he'll fall asleep. Would you mind talking to him first? It won't take long for me to get ready for bed."

"No problem."

While she headed to the bathroom to wash up, I pulled out my phone and plopped down in the odd-looking wicker chair that sat in the corner of the room. It made an ominous creaking sound but didn't break, so I figured it was safe for the moment.

"Slade, you have wonderful timing." Estrada's pleasant voice answered on the second ring. "Austin and

I were just settling in with some warm milk before he goes to bed. I have you on speaker."

"Hi, Slade!" Austin called out. "I'm drinking warm milk!"

I laughed. "That's what I hear. Were you good for Estrada?"

"Yep! I helped her wash Christmas dishes, and then we made tortillas for supper."

"He ate very well," Estrada put in.

"And I was allowed to have *two* cookies because I ate so big."

"Really? What sort of cookies did you have?"

I smiled as Austin launched into a detailed description of the iced sugar cookies that he and Estrada had made earlier in the day. They were practice cookies for the ones they'd make tomorrow to leave out for Santa. He was still explaining to me how Santa managed to eat so many cookies without getting a stomachache – something to do with him needing all that energy to deliver all the presents – when Cheyenne came out of the bathroom, wrapped up in the fluffy pink robe I'd bought her for her birthday. It had matched her hair at the time, but it still looked cute with the blue streaks.

"Hey, Austin, guess who just joined us?"

"Cheyenne!"

The joy in his voice as he yelled made me smile.

When his and Chey's mother died, Austin had been around the same age Blake had been when we lost our parents. While Cheyenne was ten times more affectionate with her brother than my grandfather had ever been with my brothers or me, I knew how fortunate we'd been to have a safe place to grow up, with more than enough of everything.

That was the life I wanted to give Cheyenne and Austin. I'd been worried at first that they wouldn't want to move across the country to join me in Boston, but they'd both been excited for a new start, especially once Estrada had agreed to join us. They'd been with me for less than a year, and I already couldn't imagine my life without them.

"Are you all tucked in?" Cheyenne asked as she made a shooing motion at me.

"Are you saying I stink?" I mouthed the words as Austin answered her question.

She stuck out her tongue, and I winked before disappearing into the bathroom. I knew she'd be a while, but I didn't bother with a shower. I enjoyed our bedtime ritual with Austin almost as much as they did. The first couple nights, I'd felt like an interloper on private family time, but then Austin had asked me to read *Hop on Pop*, and every night since then, the three of us would spend at least a few minutes all together.

I knew that some people thought I was nuts, getting involved with a woman eight years younger than me who had a kid, even if he wasn't her biological son, but there'd never been a choice for me. Even if I hadn't wanted to admit it right away, I'd been hers from the first moment I'd seen her. They were my family.

Inevitably, my thoughts went to the one Christmas present I hadn't put in the box to go under the tree tomorrow. Instead, it was tucked into a pair of my socks where I knew Chey wouldn't accidentally find it. If I'd bought her earrings, they could go under the tree with everything else. Even though it was already wrapped, no one would mistake it for anything but a ring box, especially since I'd hidden it.

My brothers wouldn't tell me that I was going too fast, not with Jax and Syll already being married, but I didn't know if Cheyenne would think it was too fast. She was still adjusting to the move and to settling into a normal routine. She'd spent so much of her life having to be the parent to both her brother and her mother, working two jobs, fending off all sorts of perverts, being exposed to things that made me wish her mother was still alive so I could put her behind bars for what she'd done to her kids.

The worst part was, I didn't know how to have the conversation that would tell me if she was in the same place as I was. How was I supposed to find out if she wanted things to stay the way they were for a while or if she'd see a proposal the same way I did. I wanted to spend the rest of my life with her, and I didn't doubt that she loved me. I just didn't know, if I got out that box and asked her the question, if she'd tell me no, or worse, say yes and not mean it.

I couldn't do it. I couldn't ask her to marry me if I wasn't one hundred percent positive that she'd say yes.

FOURTEEN
CHEYENNE

Night, December 23rd, Present Day
Hudson Valley, New York

For the hundredth time today, I told myself not to feel guilty. Estrada was part of the family. Austin spending the holiday with her was no different than kids who stayed with their grandparents or aunts and uncles while their parents had some alone time. Without any other known family on my side, and only Slade's brothers on his side, Austin didn't have much in the way of extended family, and neither did Estrada.

She'd cried when I'd told her Austin and I were moving to Boston, then cried even harder when I asked her to come with us. Since the move, Austin had started calling her *Bobe*, which he had solemnly explained to me meant that she was his granny. Apparently, one of the other little boys in the complex where we all lived called his grandmother *Bobe,* and when Austin first realized that he didn't have grandparents, he'd announced that Estrada would now be his grandmother. He'd even taken her to grandparent day at his school.

It was strange. The biggest adjustment I'd had to make in accepting Slade's invitation to move to Boston with him hadn't been the drastic Texas to Massachusetts differences, or the change in employment. It'd been realizing that I wasn't doing this alone anymore. Back in Texas, I'd needed babysitters for Austin while I worked, and even though I'd loved Estrada, I'd never felt comfortable assuming too much of her. When she'd agreed to uproot her life, it changed things for me. For the first time in my life, I had a family.

"How far did you get before he fell asleep?" Slade asked as he emerged from the bathroom.

I ignored the question and continued to ogle my boyfriend. He usually slept in just cotton or flannel pants, and I couldn't even count the number of times I'd seen him without a shirt, but he still took my breath away.

Beautiful inside and out, it was his outside I currently admired. More than a foot taller than my own five-one frame, he had the lean sort of body that came with genetics as well as conditioning. Unlike a lot of men who had muscles when they were younger, he'd maintained his physique from the army.

My gaze traced the tattoo on his chest. A cross over his heart with his parents and sister's initials on the crossbeam and the date of their death underneath. From the top of the cross, a chain went up and over his shoulder where I knew it eventually connected to a pair of dog tags on his shoulder blades. Around the dog tags was the back tattoo I'd designed for him, one that matched the alterations I'd had done to my own.

A tree losing its leaves had covered my entire back since I was eighteen. Shortly after Syll and Jax's wedding, I'd added to it. New leaves growing on the branches, each of them bearing a name of one of my new family members, with plenty of room to add more. I knew a lot of people didn't think it was a good idea to put someone's name on their body, but for me, that tattoo was made to change and adapt, to remind me of the ways my life had changed, the ways it still could.

A similar tree was on Slade's back, but instead of falling leaves, I'd incorporated his dog tags and added new ones, including one that had my name, and one for Austin. Like my design, there was plenty of room for more additions, a thought that made my stomach flutter.

It was hard to tell myself that we were moving too fast when Jax and Syll were already married, and they'd known each other only a little longer than Slade and I had. The Hunter brothers had more in common than pretty blue eyes and an amazing bone structure. When they fell, they fell hard and didn't waste any time. Well, once they finally admitted the truth to themselves.

"Are you okay?" Slade asked. "You've been staring at me for like two minutes and not saying a word." His eyes widened with alarm. "Is Austin okay?"

"He's great," I said quickly. Color flooded my cheeks. "I was just admiring you. You're sort of hot, you know?"

One dark eyebrow went up. "Only sort of?"

"We both know you're completely aware of how gorgeous you are."

He put his hand on his chest, a look of mock hurt on his face. "Are you saying that I'm vain?"

When he started to hum that oldies song, "You're So Vain," I couldn't stop myself from laughing. Then he added in a little shimmy that should've looked stupid, but all I could think was how much I wanted to lick down those deep v-grooves at his hips, and that got me laughing even harder even as it turned me on.

That was Slade. The only man who'd ever done either of those things for me.

"That's better," he said with a smile. "I like hearing you laugh."

"Laughter is good," I agreed. "Especially after a night like tonight." I sat up and held out a hand to him. "Are you okay?"

He clasped my fingers and brushed a kiss over my knuckles. "I am. It's strange, talking to my brothers like this, but it's good too. I think this was the sort of thing our grandfather had wanted for us when he put the stipulation in his will that we had to make amends with each other."

"When was the last time all four of you spent Christmas together?"

While he thought, he dropped my hand and walked around to the other side of the bed. "Three or four years, I think. I'm not even entirely sure. After Grandma Olive died, holidays pretty much blurred together."

"The Christmas after Austin turned three, our mom went out all day. She didn't say where or when she'd be back, so we had our own celebration. Estrada brought us some cookies she'd made, and we exchanged presents. Nothing big or expensive, but they were special. He'd drawn me some pictures, and I'd managed to hide some money from Mom to buy him a little stuffed animal. It was a great day." I pulled aside the blankets and sheets for him. "I'm sorry it's been so long since you had a day like that."

"It brought me to you and Austin," Slade said as he settled next to me. "That's all I need."

Now it was my turn to try to lighten the mood. "Does that mean you don't want your early present?"

His entire face lit up at my words, and for a few seconds, I could see what he must've looked like when he was Austin's age, before he'd lost so much.

I tossed the blankets down to my feet, revealing the lingerie I'd bought and smuggled into the cabin in my toiletries bag. It hadn't been difficult considering how little material there was. Sheer red lace trimmed with white fur made up the tiny thong and bra set, but it was the fur cuffs around my wrists that captured Slade's attention...until I stretched my arms over my head to draw attention to the rest of Slade's present.

"Chey." My nickname came out strangled.

"Don't worry," I addressed the one thing that I knew could keep him from enjoying what I'd done for him. "I had a woman do it."

The gold hoops in my nipples gleamed underneath the lace, as did the thin chain that connected them. I'd gotten them done a week ago and keeping them hidden from Slade hadn't been easy. They'd have to come out for a while soon enough, but there was no reason we couldn't enjoy them while we were here.

Slade was still staring when I looked up at him, and

a flicker of nervousness cut through my confidence. "Say something."

He went up on his knees and moved to straddle my waist. "Fucking perfect." Suddenly, he looked at me, eyes narrowing. "Is this why you've been keeping your shirt on the last few days?"

I licked my lips. "I wanted them to be healed enough that you could...play with them while we were here."

Slade's eyes were dark as he slid his hands up to cover my breasts. The hoops pressed against his palms, and I sucked in a breath, my back arching up into his touch. When I'd gotten them done, I hadn't realized why my nipples were already becoming more sensitive, but either way, I knew I'd enjoy what Slade would do with them. I always loved the things he did to me.

It had been strange to realize that I had a submissiveness to me that he, as a Dominant, had responded to, but his sadistic streak had been one of those things that'd made sense once I thought about it. I'd never even realized my own masochistic tendencies until he came into my life. Not damaging or extreme pain, but more than a lot of people probably would be comfortable with.

He leaned down and used his teeth to undo the bow that had been keeping the bra closed. The expression on his face as he peeled back the flimsy material was something close to reverence.

I kept as still as I could as his fingers explored, first the chain, and then the hoops, his touch feather-light. My hands curled into fists at the teasing touch, and a shiver ran down my spine. How could my entire body feel like it was on fire when we'd just barely started?

He tugged on the chain, sending jolts of pain into my nipples, and then straight down to my pussy. I whimpered and squirmed, knowing both would turn him on even more. He made a low sound in the back of his throat, then flicked one of the hoops.

"Fuck!" My entire body jerked.

"Best Christmas present ever," he said as he lowered his head to take my mouth. His fingers continued plucking and twisting the hoops, changing rhythm and force as he gauged my reactions.

He always did that. Read my body. Read my soul.

I just hoped he'd be distracted enough by my present that he wouldn't notice the tiny changes in my body, ones that I could barely find. I'd originally intended to tell him during this trip when we'd have time to discuss things without having to worry about Austin. It was going to be a shock. Hell, I'd known for nearly a whole week, and I was still trying to wrap my head around it.

I was pregnant.

I'd been on the pill, which meant it shouldn't have been possible, but nothing was ever one hundred percent. Well, technically, celibacy would've done it, but we could barely go a day without having our hands all over each other.

I just didn't know how Slade would react when I finally told him. He'd accepted Austin from moment one, which I'd always believed an impossibility. Having a high-energy five-year-old as part of a brand-new relationship wasn't easy, even for me. If I added a baby to the mix when I'd told him that we were protected, I didn't even want to imagine what he would say. I could lose him. He could tell me to terminate the pregnancy or leave. He could blame me. Hate me.

I wanted to tell him, share this with him. I wanted to be able to stop holding on to this secret. But after the way things had been going, I wasn't sure this was the best time to bring it up. Maybe later.

"Come back to me, Chey," Slade said with a sharp tug on the chain. "Or do I need to bend you over my knee and turn your ass as red as your nipples?"

Definitely later.

FIFTEEN
SLADE

MORNING, DECEMBER 24RD, PRESENT DAY

Hudson Valley, New York

I didn't realize I'd been whistling Christmas carols until Jax asked me to stop. We'd been in the attic for fifteen minutes, searching through random boxes for the Christmas ornaments that the caretaker had insisted were here. Somewhere.

"You're in a good mood this morning," he said as he opened another box. "And this is another box of newspapers."

"I thought that was sort of my thing," I said, grinning at him. "Being in a good mood."

Jax shook his head. "No, little brother, there's a good mood, and then there's whistling 'Jingle Bells' while we search a dusty attic for old Christmas ornaments. That's a whole lot of mood."

I laughed. "What can I say? I had a good night."

Understanding was almost immediate, and as soon as he spoke, I realized why.

"I thought those sounds were coming from your room last night. No soundproofing here."

"Damn, I didn't think of that." In all honesty, I hadn't thought of much of anything after I'd seen Chey's gorgeous little nipples sporting two hoops linked by a thin chain. Nothing beyond all the things I wanted to do with my new toys. Things like maybe adding a clit piercing for us both to play with.

Just the thought had my cock stiffening even though I'd spent myself inside Cheyenne twice last night and once this morning. I'd wanted to take her again in the shower after that, but I'd caught the wince she'd tried to hide. She'd never used her safe word, but I'd been with her long enough to know that she'd taken all she could get pleasure from. As her Dom, it was my responsibility to see to her pleasure. As her lover and the man who wanted to be her husband, it was my privilege to take care of and protect her.

My brother shot me an amused frown. "I don't know what you're thinking about, but you're going to have a serious case of blue balls if you don't stop because you're not going off to spend some alone time with Cheyenne until we find these damn ornaments."

I laughed and went back to our search. He was right. If I kept thinking about everything Chey and I had done since last night, I was either going to spend the whole day with an erection hard enough to cut granite or I was going to come in my pants and be teased mercilessly about it for the rest of my life. Neither choice was appealing.

By the time we found the boxes of antique-looking glass bulbs and what appeared to be a few hand-carved ornaments, Blake had returned with a beautiful Colorado Blue Spruce, easily ten feet tall. If there hadn't been a section of the living room with a vaulted ceiling, the tree never would have fit. As it was, it was a good thing we hadn't found a star for the top because it would've been too much, and none of us wanted to cut off another inch.

Syll had brought Christmas cookies and cocoa for us to enjoy while we decorated the tree, and then we all headed to our respective rooms to get our gifts. We wouldn't open anything until tomorrow morning, but we all wanted the effect of having our gifts piled under the tree tonight. I left the most important one where it was, still unsure about the timing.

Cheyenne had been so young when she'd taken on

the responsibility of raising her brother, and things hadn't changed after their mother died. When we moved here, I'd encouraged her to do things for herself and not just for me and Austin. She'd taken a few art classes and was looking into maybe going to college for an art degree. She also worked part-time at a reputable tattoo parlor, coming up with original designs.

Would she see a proposal as losing all of that? I hoped she understood me better than that, but I refused to risk this relationship on an assumption. I'd never ask her to give up the things she wanted to do with her life. In fact, I'd do whatever I could to make sure that she was given all of the opportunities that had passed her by while she'd been taking care of her brother.

None of that changed how much I wanted her to have my last name. Her and Austin both. I wanted official adoption papers so both he and Chey knew that I'd never try to split them up or make Austin feel like he wasn't as much mine as he was hers. And then I wanted to add to our family.

But I didn't want any of this if she wasn't ready for it.

I was on my way back downstairs with my gifts when a memory came to me, so sudden and clear that I stumbled. I barely managed to keep from going down face-first, but I didn't pay attention to the near-spill. I was concentrating too hard on what I'd remembered, desperate not to lose it.

A conversation between my grandparents about my parents. Those had been few and far between even when Grandma Olive had been alive. I hadn't realized I'd overheard anything important until this very moment. I must have been walking by their room for some reason or another and caught my mother's name.

"We could have stopped this, Olive," Grandfather said. *"That night he brought her here to meet us, we should have told him that we wouldn't allow the relationship to progress any further."*

"My dear," Grandma Olive's voice was soft, *"do you really think that would have done any good? We, of all people, should understand that when a Hunter finds his other half, nothing will keep them apart. He'll risk everything to be with her. Just like you did with me."*

"Slade, are you okay?" Cai asked as I lingered at the top of the stairs, trying to remember more.

I gave my head a shake. "I don't know if it's us being together or the stories you and Jax told, but I have the oddest feeling that I know what happened next with our parents."

Cai's eyebrows shot up. "Really? I thought you didn't remember much about Mom and Dad."

"I don't," I said, still thinking hard, trying to make

more of their words come to the surface. "But I think I overheard our grandparents talking about the first time they met Mom. That'd have to be the Christmas Eve party that Dad invited her to, right?"

Cai headed toward the door. "Come on, let's get everyone else together and see if we can figure it out."

I followed my brother down the stairs, half of my mind still in the past. I hoped I'd have something of my own to share, but the part I kept coming back to was my grandma's comment about how when a Hunter fell in love, he'd do anything to be with the person he loved. That's how I felt about Cheyenne, and I already knew I'd do anything to keep her.

Even if it meant holding off on my proposal to give her more time to decide what she wanted from life.

As soon as Cai announced that I'd remembered something about our parents' courtship, however, I had to put aside my own feelings and focus on the memory. I wasn't the only one hungry to know more.

Cheyenne curled up next to me, and I wrapped my arm around her even though we both knew that I was the one who needed the physical contact more than her. She grounded me in a way that nothing and no one ever had before.

I began with the same thing I'd told Cai, and before

I'd finished the sentence, the room was silent save for the fire, and everyone's attention was on me.

"Dad brought Mom to the house without telling anyone he had a date..."

SIXTEEN
CT

Evening, December 24th, 1984

New York City

I couldn't believe it. I was actually looking forward to my parents' party. That hadn't been the case since I was a kid, and even then, I'd only enjoyed the parties because I got to stay up later than my usual bedtime. Tonight, I had only one thing on my mind. Most guys would've been petrified at the thought of their parents meeting their girlfriend, but I couldn't wait to introduce Abigail to my parents.

Okay, I was a little nervous about how they might react to the fact that we'd only met yesterday, but it wasn't like she was a stripper or something. She was a nursing student at NYU who did volunteer work. I could honestly say that she wasn't pursuing me for money. She had no clue that my family was rich, though after tonight, I had no doubt she'd figure it out.

I kept repeating all of this as I walked up the stairs to Abigail's dorm room. I loved my parents, and I didn't doubt that they loved me, but I wasn't naïve about their expectations of me either. They still believed I would soon get tired of journalism and go work with my dad, and with that came the responsibility of portraying the right image to society. Which meant being attached to the right people.

I stopped at the door and counted to five before knocking. No more worrying over what my parents were going to think. If they couldn't see how special Abigail was, then that was something they'd have to learn to deal with, because I didn't intend to give her up.

"Hi, CT," she said as she opened the door.

The first thing I registered was the smile lighting up her face. Then I saw the rest of her. A simple, stylish dress of green velvet clung to every curve without being obscene. The cut was entirely modest, and somehow that made her even more attractive. Part of me wanted to tell her to forget the party. We'd stay in and spend our time wrapped up in each other, whether figuratively or literally.

"You're beautiful," I said, reaching for her hand. When I kissed her knuckles, she blushed, reminding me of how her skin had flushed last night when we'd been in the car. Not for the first time in the last twenty-four hours, I wondered how far that blush would go.

"You clean up well," she replied, giving my fingers a squeeze before releasing me. "Did you want to come in?"

"Do you want me to?"

An awkward pause hung between us for several seconds, long enough for me to think that I'd made a mistake coming here, asking her to come to this party with me. I was still trying to figure out the best way to break the silence when she did it for me.

"My place is a mess. If you don't mind, we can go straight to your party."

I nodded. "Grab a coat. It's cold out there."

She smiled at me, warming me straight down to my toes. "Always looking out for me."

It should have been strange that barely twenty-four hours had set up 'always,' but somehow it wasn't. With anyone else, all the things I'd felt since I'd seen her scarf catch fire would have terrified me. With her, I simply wanted more.

I held out my arm, and she took it, letting me lead her down the three flights of stairs to the lobby. I'd rented a car for us since I hadn't wanted to make her walk or ride public transportation in a nice dress and heels. I could have asked my parents to send a car, but that wasn't how I wanted her to find out about who my parents were. Still, I knew I had to tell her before she met them.

I waited until we were halfway there to bring it up. "Remember how you asked me about having a house in the Hamptons?" I glanced her way, and she nodded. "*I* don't. I was an NYU student, and I have a place in the city. My parents, however, do have a house in the Hamptons. A big one. Not as big as our family home in Boston, but big enough."

She blinked, turning more fully toward me. "Are you trying to tell me that you're rich?"

I allowed myself a half-smile. "I'm not. My family is."

"You're sounding pretty insistent on the distinction between you and your family." Her voice was mild, impossible to read.

"It's a distinction a lot of people don't see," I said, gripping the steering wheel tighter, hoping I could explain this right. "I grew up with Hunter Enterprises looming over me. Everyone expected me to make that my life too, but it wasn't what I wanted."

"How did your parents take that?"

"They weren't happy about it, and I don't think they've really accepted it, even now, but it's better than it was when I went off to college."

"They didn't disinherit you or something like that?"

I shook my head. "No, they didn't cut me off or anything so final. They helped with college, that sort of thing, but I work too."

"You didn't tell me this yesterday."

"People can get weird when they know my family has money." I waited to hear if my omission would ruin things, but she smiled at me.

"I get it. Sometimes, it's difficult for people to look past their perceptions and biases."

I reached over and took her hand, my skin humming where it touched hers. She didn't need to say it for me to know that we were in this together. She wasn't going to leave me hanging tonight, and she wasn't going to suck up to my parents because she knew who they were now. It was the best start I could hope for.

My parents were generous donors to various museums and art galleries in both New York and Boston, and every Christmas Eve, they chose one of the buildings to host their party. This one was smaller than ones in the past, but the sculptures and artwork inside were beautiful.

Not as beautiful as Abigail though. Half the men in the room had been watching her since we'd arrived a few minutes ago. Now, as we approached my parents, even more eyes turned our way.

"Chester." My mother saw me first and stepped around the governor who was still talking to my father.

"Mother." I leaned down to let her kiss my cheeks the same way she always had. "You look lovely."

"Thank you." She patted my cheek, and I managed not to roll my eyes.

"Mother, I'd like you to meet Abigail Slade, my date tonight." I reached back to take Abigail's hand. "Abigail, my mother, Olive Hunter."

"Mrs. Hunter, it's a pleasure to meet you." Abigail was polite as she held out her hand to greet my mother.

"I'm surprised you made it tonight, Chester," my father cut in with his hand out. "No big stories for you to be chasing?"

"Not tonight," I said, forcing my teeth not to grind. "Father, this is Abigail Slade. Abigail, my father, Manfred Hunter."

"Hello." He shook her hand politely enough, but it was clear that was all he was being.

Which was pretty much what I'd expected, honestly.

"That's a lovely dress." Mother offered a smile with her compliment.

"Thank you."

The small talk went back and forth between the two as Father and I awkwardly stood at their sides. Usually, during conversations that involved someone more than just the two of them, my parents worked in tandem, but the problem here was that my father and I hadn't had anything to talk about in a long time. He didn't understand my chosen profession, and I didn't understand why he placed such an importance on the family business. It wasn't like it was anything world-changing.

When he cleared his throat, I knew the conversation was coming to an end.

"While it's been good talking to you, Miss Slade, we need to see to our other guests as well. Enjoy the remainder of your evening."

And with that, he took my mother's elbow, and the two went on their way. I didn't bother to watch them go. Father had been telling the truth that they were going to talk to their other guests. That was their thing. Somewhere nearby were guests far more important than us.

"That went pretty much how I expected," I said. "Come on, let's get something to drink."

"Um, I'm only nineteen," Abigail said, cheeks turning pink. "The drinking age went up to twenty-one, remember?"

"THEN WE'LL GORGE ourselves on food and sparkling cider instead," I said, running a hand down the soft velvet of her arm. "I don't want to be accused of corrupting the innocent."

As we headed over to the elaborate buffet, I slid my arm around her waist. My heart gave an unsteady thump when she leaned into me, and I accepted the fact that, despite the short amount of time I'd known her, I'd fallen head-over-heels in love with Abigail Slade.

SEVENTEEN
ABIGAIL

EVENING, DECEMBER 24ᵀᴴ, 1984

New York City

This was not at all how my life was supposed to go. Sure, I'd toyed with the idea of getting married, but it had been something in the far-off future, not really on my radar yet. I never imagined that it was because I hadn't met the right man until a stupid party in the Hamptons.

I kept telling myself that it was crazy to think this way. Aside from the fact that it'd probably scare him away, I couldn't possibly know what I wanted from whatever this was between us. I was practical. I believed in logic and science. Other women could have flights of fancy when it came to relationships and love. Not me.

Why, then, did my heart feel like it was about ready

to explode when all he'd done was take my hand? How could I tell myself that this wasn't racing forward, threatening to hurtle me off a cliff when I'd been ready to have sex with him after knowing him for only a few hours? And in a car, for that matter. Everything I'd ever believed told me that this was impossible, but everything I was feeling said that this was real.

"Are you all right?" CT asked, his voice gentle as he leaned closer to me.

I read the concern in his eyes, on his face, and knew that he didn't think I was ill. He was worried that meeting his family had freaked me out. I wasn't foolish enough to believe that they thought I was anything more than a date for tonight, but I certainly wasn't going to allow myself to believe anything other than the same thing. I would make no assumptions, hold no expectations.

"I'm well, thank you," I said with a smile. "Nothing's wrong."

"Are you sure? I know this can be a lot to take in, especially when I didn't warn you ahead of time..."

I placed my hand on his cheek, effectively stopping what I was sure would've ended up being an apology for bringing me here in the first place. It seemed the confident young man who'd bordered on being cocky wasn't as sure of himself all the time as he pretended to be.

"I'm fine. I promise." I met his gaze with a steady one of my own. "If I wasn't, I'd tell you. Now, what do you say we check out the dessert table?"

He smiled, those beautiful pale blue eyes of his lighting up. I liked to think I wasn't a shallow person, but I couldn't deny how insanely hot CT was. Most of the women here had been alternating between checking him out and shooting daggers at me, even though the majority of those women had been closer to his mother's age than his own. He was either oblivious or used to the attention because he didn't acknowledge any of it.

"Desserts. You're talking my language." He rested his hand at the small of my back and steered us through the crowd toward the table weighed down with all sorts of fancy sweets, all of which were barely a mouthful.

"They almost look too pretty to eat," I commented as I took in the array of tarts, truffles, and cheesecakes. Cookies, cakes, and candy. Chocolates, fruits, nuts, meringue...

I felt like I'd stepped into Willy Wonka's chocolate factory.

"I've never been a fan of a lot of the fancy food served at parties like this," CT said. "Caviar, escargot, that sort of thing, I have to choke down. But there's always a great spread for dessert. People like this like to pretend they're above having a sweet tooth, that a single bite is good enough, but don't let them fool you. Most of them will make a dozen trips, taking only one thing at a time so they can appear to be all dignified while they're secretly stuffing their faces."

I laughed, unable to stop myself. "You seem awfully cynical about some cookies and treats."

He had the grace to look a bit embarrassed. "Sorry. That's the part people don't really get about growing up with all this. I can acknowledge how fortunate I've been, but still see how fake everything is."

I picked up something that looked like a mini macaroon. "Do you have any food allergies?"

He looked surprised before he shook his head, but not even close to as surprised as he was when I shoved the entire cookie into his mouth.

"More eating, less talking."

"THANK you for coming with me tonight," he said as he opened the passenger door for me.

"Thank you for inviting me," I replied, carefully swinging my legs into the car, knees pressed firmly together.

He started the car almost immediately after getting in, turning the heat up full blast, but didn't put the car in drive. "I usually get roped into a couple of these a year. I don't really like them, but they help keep my dad off my back about coming to work with him."

I didn't understand where he was going with this, but I kept silent as I waited for him to continue.

"I've never taken anyone with me, and I've never cared what anyone thought about my family." He reached over and took my hand. "I wasn't looking for this when I agreed to go with Finn yesterday. All I was hoping for was an end to him constantly trying to set me up. Maybe good conversation if I was lucky."

"I know what you mean," I admitted. My pulse was flying again. "I didn't expect this, whatever this is between us."

"I don't think I can give it up," he said softly. "And if I'm being honest, I don't want to."

"Me either." I could barely get the words out. I'd never even considered that he might be feeling the same thing I was.

"I'll slow down." His thumb moved back and forth across my knuckles. "If that's what you want. What you need. Just, please, don't walk away."

"I'm not going anywhere," I promised, sandwiching his hand between both of mine, holding on as though he was the single thing that could keep me from floating away. "I feel like I'm falling, rushing headlong into something that's going to consume me...but I'm not scared as long as you're right there with me."

"I am," he assured me. "This thing between us, it's the most real thing I've ever felt."

"Me too."

He reached up to tuck some hair behind my ear. "I'm not ready for tonight to end."

A shiver went down my spine. "Me either."

"It's okay if you want me to take you home. I meant what I said, about us going at your speed. But I don't want to hide anything." His fingers brushed across my cheek, and he waited. "Especially not when it comes to how I feel about you."

After how hot and heavy things had gotten between us last night, I had no doubt what would happen if I told him that I wasn't ready for us to part ways tonight either. Unless we went someplace public, CT and I would end up in bed together. I wanted that, without apology and without excuse, but I knew his honesty had to be matched with my own. If we were going to do this tonight, he had to know what to expect.

"I don't want to go home yet," I said, my voice more steady than I thought it'd be.

"Do you...want to see my place?" His fingers tightened around my hand.

I nodded. "But there's something you need to know

first." I barely waited a beat before blurting it out, "I'm a virgin."

His eyes went wide, but only for a fraction of a second. "I have to be honest with you," he said, color flooding his face. "I'm not."

"I didn't expect you to be," I said in a rush. "And I don't want to make a big thing out of it. It's just that if things go that far tonight, I didn't want you to be, well, surprised."

"We don't have to go that far."

I leaned over and kissed his cheek. "Thank you for saying that...but I want to. I wanted to last night. Just not in a car."

He laughed, a warm, full sound that made my insides squirm pleasantly. "No, you definitely deserve better than a car."

I called up my best mischievous grin. "For tonight anyway. I'm not opposed to fooling around in a car in the future."

He stared at me, irises going heated and dark. "Please don't say things like that when I'm driving, or we'll end up in another ditch."

It was my turn to laugh, and the sound carried with it the undercurrent of arousal I felt through every inch of me. I loved that I could affect him that much. I loved that he wasn't going to pressure me into anything I didn't want to do.

And I had the strangest feeling that I'd already fallen in love with him.

By the time we reached his place, I was certain of it.

"You should have seen this place when Hunter Enterprises first bought it," CT said as he led me up the front steps and into the lobby. "I made a deal with my dad in high school that I'd work part-time for the company if I could choose the department. I did some office work the first two years. Then, junior year, we bought this building. It was falling apart. Dangerous. I decided I wanted to work with the construction crews hired to fix this place up. One of the things that's always set us apart from other businesses like us is that we don't outsource. We have our own crews – electricians, plumbers, construction guys, specialists, you name it – and they never have to worry about lulls. We always have something for them to do."

We stepped onto an ancient-looking elevator, and CT pressed the button for the top floor.

"Anyway, I worked my ass off on this place, enjoying the research and restoration as much as the physical work. The piece I wrote about progress and the loss of history was what got me into the journalism program at NYU. And it got my name to the right people at the *Times*. I wrote it because of this place."

I loved the way he was telling his story. Pride at the work he did, and the people his family's company employed, without a hint of false modesty or apology.

"When I told my parents I was going to NYU, I wasn't worried about paying for school because my grandparents had set aside money for me for college, and it was completely my choice where to go. I planned on living on campus to save money for an apartment after I graduated. My dad surprised me though. He said he knew how much I loved this building, and he'd just sold it. He introduced me to the new owner who offered me the top-floor loft rent-free if I managed the place."

My jaw dropped as I stepped off the elevator and into a beautifully renovated loft. I wasn't much of a fan of the current home décor or architectural trends, which meant this classic look was exactly the sort of thing I loved.

A skylight. Wide, open spaces that included the kitchen, living room, and bedroom. Only the bathroom appeared to be closed off. It wasn't as messy as I would've thought a bachelor pad would be, but the little things here and there made it lived-in.

"This is so much better than my dorm room," I said, turning in circles to take it all in. "And definitely better than the front seat of a borrowed car."

He laughed as he caught me around the waist, the

sound cutting off as his mouth came down on mine. Here was the hunger and heat we'd experienced last night, and now we had no reason to stop. No one would interrupt us. Whatever we did would be because we both wanted it.

And to hell with anyone who had a problem.

Our clothes dropped to the floor with barely a whisper, our lips moving together even as he walked me backward toward his bed. We fell in a tangle of limbs, skin against skin, hands exploring as sensation threatened to overwhelm. My brain struggled to process each new bit of information.

His palm skimmed my breasts, and I gasped into his mouth.

Our tongues danced together as I buried my fingers in his hair.

A large hand palmed one ass cheek, squeezed.

My nails scraped over one taut nipple, and he cursed.

I was on my back, and he leaned over me, hands on either side of my shoulders. When he kissed his way down between my breasts, then took the time to tease my aching nipples with his mouth, I squirmed under him. I'd never felt a need like this before. Vast and all-consuming, as if nothing could meet it.

His fingers slipped between my thighs, and my hips

jerked. I closed my eyes, fingers curling at the pleasure rippling out from where he stroked me. I was so turned on that I was practically dripping, but I couldn't find the energy to be embarrassed by it.

"Damn, baby." CT's voice was hoarse. "Are you that wet for me?"

I nodded, then moaned as a shudder went through me. I was a virgin, but I'd explored my own body enough to know that I was going to come soon. He kept talking, encouraging me, coaxing me further along the edge, and then slipped a finger inside. He cursed, easing his finger in and out until my muscles relaxed and he could insert a second finger. The entire time, his thumb didn't stop moving back and forth across my clit, building that pressure inside me until I finally came with a shout.

My muscles were still quivering when CT settled between my legs, but my eyes and mind were clear when he asked me if I was sure. I answered him by wrapping my legs around his waist, resting my heels on the backs of his knees. The tip of him brushed against me, and his eyes closed.

"You're going to kill me," he said, voice strained.

I swept his hair back from his face, my hand lingering on his cheek. "I will if you don't get inside me soon."

He opened his eyes as he entered me, inching his

way forward until his pelvis rested on mine. My breathing came in harsh, desperate gasps and my hands shook. I didn't have that sharp, tearing pain that I'd always heard about, but I was a nurse. I knew anatomy well enough to know that the full, tight discomfort was natural, and it would pass as I relaxed.

I was surprised at how easy it was to do just that, but even that melted away as CT rocked back, and then forward. The heat between us sparked into flame, flowing over our skin, between us, around us, creating a cocoon of brilliance that grew brighter and brighter until it shattered, and we shattered with it.

If I hadn't accepted it before, I knew it now. I was in love with CT Hunter, and my life was never going to be the same.

EIGHTEEN
BLAKE

EVENING, DECEMBER 24RD, PRESENT DAY
Hudson Valley, New York

"Grandma Olive said that she watched them at the party," Slade said, "and by the time they left, she knew that Dad and Mom were meant to be together. She told Grandfather that if he would've listened to her then, he wouldn't have wasted so much time trying to change things."

Silence filled the room as Slade finished talking and we all worked on this new information.

I'd spent the months since meeting Brea dealing with all of the emotions I'd stuffed down for twenty-five years, but even with the woman I loved at my side, the anger hadn't gone easily. Sometimes, it even came back with a vengeance I didn't expect.

Like now.

How could our grandparents have kept stories like this from us? How could they have stood by, day by day, and not realized that their stories of our parents were all some of us had? Maybe Grandma Olive had had a legitimate excuse to wait. We'd been children, grieving the losses of our parents and sister. Grandfather though, he'd had more than two decades to tell us what he knew, and he'd kept it all to himself.

"I can't believe I didn't remember that before," Slade said, reaching over to take Cheyenne's hand. "All this time, that memory's been in my head."

"You shouldn't have needed to be the one to tell us," I said, struggling to keep my voice even. "Grandfather should have told us. He should have made sure we knew all about them."

Brea leaned against my shoulder, and her presence steadied me.

"We should have talked about them more," Jax said. "I'm sorry about that, Blake."

"We can't change the past," Cai said, "but we can try to make things better."

Jax nodded, concern lining his forehead. "Cai's right. We'll talk about them, tell you what we remember." He held Syll tighter. "We'll tell you all what we remember."

Another minute of silence followed his pronounce-
ment, and then Syll broke it. "I think this has been
enough for tonight. It's getting late." She smiled widely,
but she couldn't completely hide the strain around her
eyes. "Besides, Santa won't come if we don't go to sleep."

Slade laughed, and it was a familiar sound, an old
sound. He was falling into his previous role as the easy-
going brother, the one who diffused the tension with
jokes and laughter. The flash of pain in his eyes was
quick, but I saw it.

"No, Slade." I leaned forward and looked at each of
my brothers in turn. I wasn't eloquent, but I would get
my point across. "We're not going to fall back into bad
habits, blaming each other, pretending. I don't want to
be that person again, and I don't think any of you do
either."

Cai got up and came over to where I was sitting. He
crouched down in front of me. "You're right. We won't
just shove all this aside, I promise."

"We all promise," Slade said, relief written across his
face. He stood and held out his hand to Cheyenne. "But
Mrs. Hunter over there has the right idea. Let's call it a
night, have a nice Christmas, and then start tackling this
stuff again."

No one else said much of anything, but we did
follow his advice, each of us making our way back to our

rooms in virtual silence. I didn't know how much the others were talking about what had just happened, but I didn't want to talk about it at all.

One of the things I loved the most about my beautiful fiancée was that she had the uncanny ability to know when to push me and when to let me work through things for a bit on my own. Right now, I needed some time on my own, and Brea let me have it when she claimed the bathroom first.

This wasn't right. That was the thought that kept going around and around in my head. But as my anger faded, I began to realize that the thing nagging at me wasn't because of my grandparents or my brothers or the stories I didn't know. Something was...off.

"Are you okay?" Brea asked as she came out of the bathroom, a concerned expression on her face.

"Just thinking," I said as I took her in my arms and let the familiar feel of her body, the scent of her, ease me.

I wondered if I'd ever touch her and not wonder how I'd managed to find this woman. She believed in fate and destiny, but I'd never even considered those possibilities until she came into my life. There was no other explanation for why this gorgeous, brilliant, sweet woman loved me. Why she was wearing my ring and carrying my child. Our wedding would be New Year's Day in Boston, our honeymoon an Alaskan cruise, and then back to Rawlins, Wyoming. We'd probably visit Boston once more before our baby's birth this summer, but our life would always be centered in our home in Wyoming.

"Was it a mistake to come here?" I asked, the words muffled as I kissed the top of Brea's head. Her raven-black curls were soft against my lips.

"No." She tipped her head back, and I let myself fall into the dark pools of her eyes.

I'd never known that a woman could hold sway over me, but from the moment I first met her, I'd been captivated. I'd also been pissed, but the fact that my anger hadn't scared her away had only set her apart from anyone else I'd ever known.

"You can't believe this was a mistake," she said, reaching up to put her hands on my cheeks. "The memories are going to hurt, but you'll never forgive yourself if you push everyone away again."

"I know."

I buried one hand in those wonderful curls and dropped the other to Brea's firm ass. She ground her hips against me, and I slammed my mouth down on hers. She pushed up on her tiptoes, her tongue battling mine even as her hands moved under my shirt, nails raking across my skin.

I wanted nothing more than to push her against the wall and be inside her. A few quick moments were all it would take, and I could lose myself in her. She wanted it too. Her mouth was demanding, her hands eager. Her nipples were hard bullets through her filmy nightgown. The new, slight swell of her belly only fueled my desire. Not that there was anything that could make me not want her. It was like a physical ache, this need.

Then her hands were pushing instead of pulling, and I immediately released her. She hadn't used our safe word, but I'd felt the urgency in her touch. I took a step back, far enough to give her space, but close enough that I could react if she needed me.

Her eyes were closed, one hand on her stomach, the other on her mouth.

"Are you okay?" It was my turn to ask her the question, this one more urgent with concern.

She nodded, and I waited with her, trusting her to tell me if there was anything I could do. Her morning sickness hadn't quite gotten the memo about what time of day it was supposed to appear. It came and went without any sort of pattern, and while it didn't last long, when it hit, it hit sharp and fast.

Finally, she opened her eyes and offered me a weak smile. "Rain check?"

"Of course," I said as I reached for her, my sole focus now on comfort rather than sex.

I hated seeing her sick and hated even more the fact

that it was my fault. How women survived this more than once, I'd never know. That had been one of my biggest fears since I'd learned she was pregnant: that the pregnancy would make her resent me and I'd lose her.

If I was completely honest, even the moment I'd proposed had been filled with similar fear. Her parents had raised her in an unconventional, open, free-love environment, and while she'd never embraced that lifestyle, I couldn't help wondering if the idea of a more-or-less traditional family was simply a 'grass is greener' mentality. A daydream she only *thought* she wanted.

What if, after we got married and the baby came, and she realized it would be just me and her for the rest of our lives, she decided that her parents had it right after all. What if she wanted more than I could give her?

What if I wasn't enough?

NINETEEN
BREA

NIGHT, DECEMBER 24RD, PRESENT DAY

Hudson Valley, New York

I splashed more cool water on my face and concentrated on my breathing. The bouts of nausea I'd been having – no 'morning' sickness for me – were intense, but mercifully brief. Mint tea sometimes helped but I didn't think I'd need it this time. I was already starting to feel better. Still, I stayed in the bathroom a bit longer, embarrassment and frustration warring for the top spot.

Blake had been amazing these past couple months. People who only knew him as the gruff, often foul-mouthed recluse who preferred horses to people wouldn't have believed how gentle and tender my fiancé could be. A muscular six feet four inches, he could look every bit the scary mountain man, but from the moment

I'd told him I was pregnant, he'd handled me with kid gloves.

While I appreciated all he was doing to take care of me, I missed the rough, dominating man who'd introduced me to a world of pleasure I'd only heard about. I'd asked my doctor specific questions to ensure that nothing would harm the baby, but even with that, Blake had refused anything that wasn't soft and sweet. I enjoyed that sort of making love, but he and I had been brought together with the kind of passion and fire that ignited infernos.

When I thought about how he'd taken me the first time, on his kitchen counter during our first date, it twisted things inside me. I wanted that back. For a few minutes, I'd thought I would finally have it again, but my stomach had had other ideas. Even if I went back out there and told him I felt fine, he'd insist on coddling me.

In the logical part of my brain, I understood where he was coming from. Losing his parents and twin at such a young age had traumatized him more than he'd even acknowledge, especially considering he'd been in the car when it'd happened. Survivor's guilt wasn't strong enough to describe what Blake had been experiencing the last twenty-five years. Even though he'd never put it into words, I knew he was terrified that something would happen to me and the baby. He'd never forgive himself if anything he did hurt us.

That was logic, and it should have been what I listened to, but common sense wasn't being particularly friendly to me lately.

The closer we got to our wedding, the more often dark thoughts plagued me. One especially strong one was coming through loud and clear right now.

I wasn't going to be enough for him.

Our relationship had more to it than sex, but the physical attraction between us had always been strong, even when we'd been furious with each other. We'd had difficulties staying away from each other almost from the moment we'd first met, and it hadn't taken long after that for Blake to share the less vanilla side of his sexual needs. Needs that hadn't been getting met recently.

I'd watched my parents live their unconventional lives, and it had always seemed to work for them. They'd never legally married and had taken other lovers over the years, sometimes together, sometimes not, but they'd never separated. That had never been the life I'd wanted for myself, though, and I thought I'd found my one and only in Blake.

But now I wasn't as confident that I was what he needed.

How long would he be able to deny the need he had

to completely let go, to dominate in all the ways he needed? How long until he approached our relationship in the same way my parents came to theirs? Would he meet someone first and then ask me about opening up our marriage? Or would he not even want to go through with the wedding, deciding instead that it would be better for both of us if we modeled ourselves after Blair and Kevin? After all, they'd been together for decades.

"Brea, are you okay in there?" Blake's concern warmed me, but I didn't want to be warm. I wanted to be hot. Burning. Consumed by the fire we used to have.

I blinked back tears and scolded myself for letting my emotions run away with me. Blake hadn't even hinted that he wanted something other than what we had. I was only hurting myself by speculating.

"I'll be right out." I was surprised at how strong and steady my voice was.

I gave myself another minute and then pushed down all of my doubts and worries. Blake needed me to be there for him right now. My own insecurities could wait. Maybe all these crazy pregnancy hormones would straighten themselves out, and I wouldn't have to deal with any of the rest of it.

"Do you need anything?" Blake asked as soon as I came out of the bathroom. "Mint tea? Crackers?"

I shook my head and gave him the best smile I could manage. "I'm already feeling better."

That was the truth, physically at least. If I laid down for a few minutes, I'd be fine. I was lucky to have such a simple solution, I reminded myself as I made my way over to the bed. I'd always considered myself an optimistic person, and it bothered me that I struggled with finding the good in this.

As Blake and I lay side by side, staring up at the ceiling in the dark, I couldn't find the positive in this gulf between us. Our arms were touching, and I could feel the heat of him under the blanket, but neither one of us made a move toward the other. I ached for him to hold me again, to curl my body into his and have his arms around me, but I couldn't bring myself to make the first move. If he needed space and rejected me, the thin protective shell I'd formed around me would crack.

"I keep thinking about Cai's story."

I turned my head toward Blake, surprised that he'd spoken first.

"Something's off about it." I heard the frown in his voice. "Not like Cai's lying about it, but like there's something missing. A piece of the puzzle I know but can't quite find."

"Do you think talking to your brothers will help?" I asked.

"No." He blew out a long breath. "I think it's going to be like what happened before. I need something to jar my memory loose."

He didn't have to explain what he meant. It hadn't been that long ago when his subconscious had revealed a memory he hadn't realized still lingered there. It'd been that memory that had finally revealed the truth behind the wreck that had killed Chester, Abigail, and Aimee Hunter. That it hadn't been an accident but rather a calculated strike against Mr. Hunter, who'd been writing a story about some dirty dealings in a pharmaceutical company.

While Blake had been grateful for the answers, it had been horrible for him to remember that he'd actually seen his mother and sister dead. I hoped that whatever his mind was trying to bring forward wouldn't be nearly as traumatic.

"Did you hear anything about what's up in the attic?" he asked, his body going stiff. "I mean, did Jax or Slade say anything about if they found other stuff in the attic besides the decorations?"

"Syll said something about there being boxes of papers and things like that, but the guys didn't really look through them."

Where was he going with this?

"Nothing about this makes any sense," he said.

"Grandma Olive buys a cabin, tells no one about it, but arranges for the grounds to be maintained, and puts a bunch of random boxes in the attic, including Christmas ornaments."

He was right, but he didn't need me to say it out loud. This was his way of whistling in the dark, so to speak. I'd actually heard him talking to the horses like this too, though he said he did that less since we'd been together.

"Grandfather might have known about it, or he might not have. He never took Grandma Olive's name off of any of the accounts, not even when he added Jax's name to the business ones."

I sometimes wondered if Blake and his brothers ever thought about the person their grandfather would've been if things had been different. Their own lives would have changed drastically, but did they realize that their grandfather might've been different too?

"Either way," Blake continued, "it seems strange that either of them would've used the attic here to store junk. Which means those boxes were probably put there on purpose, specifically chosen to be brought here and put in the attic."

If we'd been talking about my parents, I wouldn't have thought any of this meant anything, but that was because my parents were – as much as I loved them –

flakes. They wouldn't have had the sort of forethought needed to make those types of decisions. Not even my father, who'd once been a businessman almost as successful as Manfred Hunter. Kevin was more contacts and charm than organization and business savvy.

The entire Hunter family, however, were planners. As far as I could tell, Blake was the most impulsive of them, and even he would've thought things through when it came to what to put in a vacation home.

"We should check those boxes out," I suggested.

"You think?"

"I do," I answered honestly. "You should explore every inch of this place before we leave. Who knows what you could find."

I blinked as the light came on. Blake was sitting up in bed, something of a lost boy in his expression. "I want to go now."

I didn't look at the clock and tell him that it was too late. I didn't recommend that he wait until his brothers woke up so they could go with him. None of those suggestions would help him. He needed to do this now, and I needed to do it with him.

"Let me grab my robe."

"You don't have to come."

"You might want to put on a shirt," I said as a

response to his statement. "I doubt the attic is very insulated."

When he helped me from the ladder to the attic floor, I immediately noticed that I was right. Not much in the way of insulation. Our breath puffed out in white mist, glowing eerily in the cold white light of the flashlight Blake had grabbed. Any warmth the sun might've provided had been leeched away hours ago.

"Any idea where to start?" I asked. "We should have a system to keep us from going through something twice."

He grinned at me. "Systematic organization? At least some of my good qualities are rubbing off on you."

I rolled my eyes and turned my attention to the closest box. The space wasn't packed, but there were still a fair number of boxes for us to go through. If we wasted time talking, we'd be here until sunrise.

We moved in relative quiet, focusing all of our attention on the boxes' contents rather than talking to each other unless we found something interesting. While some newspaper articles might've interested me on a normal day, I set them aside without a second glance and moved on to the next one. We'd been working for nearly half an hour when Blake said my name.

I went to his side and immediately saw the reason he'd called me over. In his hands, he held a fireproof box.

Not a new one, but an older model with what appeared to be a broken lock. While I supposed it was possible that the box was simply being used to store more newspapers and magazine articles, my gut told me that this was important.

As soon as he lifted the lid, my suspicions were confirmed. I didn't even need to look at him to know that we'd found something.

TWENTY
BLAKE

MORNING, DECEMBER 25ᵀᴴ, PRESENT DAY

Hudson Valley, New York

I'd considered not waiting to show the others what I'd found, but Brea's cooler head had prevailed. We'd carried the box back to our room, then taken a hot shower to relax us both, even though I doubted I'd be totally relaxed as long as we weren't at home. Back in bed, I'd held her until she'd fallen asleep, and then I managed to drift off for a while.

On her advice, I kept silent through an absolutely delicious breakfast, and then through our gift exchange. Fortunately, being a naturally taciturn person meant that no one thought it strange that I barely said anything beyond a general 'thank you' for each of my gifts. They were all great, and being here with my brothers and the women we all loved was more than I'd ever imagined I could have.

I only hoped that they'd see what I had the same way I did. As something good, if a bit sad.

After we ended the family video call with Austin and Estrada, Brea nodded at me, and I cleared my throat. All eyes turned to me, and Brea slipped her hand into mine, giving it a reassuring squeeze.

"Listening to you guys talk about Mom and Dad got me thinking. You know how I finally remembered about the crash?" I rubbed my jaw with my free hand. "Well, I remembered something else about that day."

Everything went still. I couldn't even hear the others breathing as they waited for me to share.

"They were talking about their anniversary, and I remember Mom saying something about how they needed to decide when to tell us the truth about when they got married. She said Grandfather and Grandma Olive would understand now. Dad said he wanted to wait until our first Christmas at the cabin. They only had a couple more payments before it was theirs, free and clear."

"This cabin?" Jax's words came out choked with emotion. "They were buying..."

"Blake and I went looking in the attic, and we found this." Brea picked up the fireproof box. "It was already unlocked."

"Jax and I didn't see that in the attic," Slade said. "What's in it?"

"The original paperwork to the cabin." I opened the box and pulled out the sheaf of paper on top. I held it out to Jax. "It's all there. Rental details that list our parents as doing a rent to own thing for six years, as well as what looks like their first time renting it the day after Christmas for four days – two years and six months before Jax was born."

"At least the whole cabin thing makes more sense now," Slade said. "Our grandparents never talked about anything that had to do with our parents."

"The cabin thing's interesting," Addison interjected, "but isn't anyone going to mention the *other* part of the conversation? About their marriage?"

"The timing's odd, but it's not exactly a shock," Cai said. "We now know they met before Christmas and were together for six months before they got married. A bit quick, but nothing crazy."

I didn't say anything as I took two more things out of the box. One was an envelope with our names on it; the other was a single rectangular piece of paper. I set them on the table and waited for my brothers to look over both. Neither one was going to offer the same sort of revelation that we'd experienced when we'd learned the truth about our parents' and sister's deaths, but they each had new information about the people we'd lost.

TWENTY-ONE
CT

Morning, December 25th, 1984

New York City

I'd never woken up next to a woman on Christmas Day before. Hell, I'd rarely woken up next to anyone at all. I tended to be more of the 'make an excuse to leave right after' kind of guy. And I definitely didn't take women back to my place for the night. With Abigail, it hadn't even felt weird.

I lay perfectly still, watching her sleep. Her dark hair was tousled, covering part of her face as she rested her cheek on my chest. One of her hands was curled over my heart, and her soft breasts pushed against my ribcage. Every inch of her delicious body was bare, the warm silk of her skin slipping across mine as she shifted in her sleep.

My cock stiffened, unneeded evidence that I wanted her again. I wouldn't take her though, not yet. She'd been a virgin until last night, and while she'd assured me that I hadn't hurt her, I didn't want to risk making love to her again when she was most likely sore. I'd wait.

It was easier to make that decision than I'd thought it would be. Probably because I already knew that I was in this for the long haul. And not simply a week or month or year. I couldn't imagine my life without her. Hell, I could barely remember a life before her, and we'd only been together a couple of days.

I needed her to understand that.

I brushed my fingers over her hair, admiring the rich color, the soft texture. I could spend hours just looking at her. I was barely aware of time passing, but then she stirred, and the world started up again. I didn't mind though, not as long as she was next to me.

"Morning." I brushed a kiss against the top of her head. "Did you sleep well?"

"I did," she said, her voice foggy with sleep. "Did you?"

"I did," I echoed. "But I'm also enjoying being awake."

She laughed, ducking her head against my shoulder. "Is it always like this?"

"Is what always like this?" I asked the question even

though I was fairly certain I knew what she meant.

"The morning after."

I had a feeling she was blushing.

"Is this what it's like, waking up in someone's arms?"

"I wouldn't know," I admitted. "I've never cared about someone enough to do it before."

She looked up at that, her eyes big and shining. "You care about me?"

I had a choice here. I could choose a half-truth – that I *cared* about her – or I could bare it all. I'd never gotten anywhere by playing it safe, and I didn't intend to do it now.

I hooked my finger under her chin to keep her from looking away. "I love you."

The shock registered first, but it only lasted as long as it took to be replaced by something so intense that it made my stomach twist.

"I love you too."

I should've been wary of a woman who was that quick to declare her devotion, but she didn't have an ounce of deception in her. My parents would need more than my belief before they trusted that she wasn't a gold digger, but their opinions were concerns for another time. Right now, the two of us were all that mattered.

"Marry me."

Her jaw dropped. "What?"

I smiled as she scrambled upright, grabbing at the sheet to cover herself as she settled on her knees. "Easy." I held up my hands, palms out. "I don't need an answer right now. It's okay. I just need you to know that I mean it. I want to marry you. Whenever and wherever you're ready. I'm all in."

"Really?" She raised an eyebrow. "You think you can just spout off some pretty words and that's all it'll take?"

She sounded curious rather than mad.

"I think you're far too smart to believe pretty words." I'd never said anything more honest in my life. "And I think you know that I'm telling the truth. I love you, and I want to marry you. No matter how crazy it sounds, no matter how insane people will think I am, that's the truth. I know it in my gut, in my bones."

She stared at me for a minute, and I let her, knowing that she needed to come to an understanding herself. When she smiled, a sense of relief went through me. She hadn't run away.

"If you're really that committed, then we should get married as soon as we can get in front of a judge."

The twinkle in her eyes made me think that she was partially teasing me, challenging me. My parents would be furious, but I didn't care. This wasn't about them. It was about me and Abigail.

"I agree." I sat up. "Let me make a few calls."

TWENTY-TWO
ABIGAIL

Morning, December 26th, 1984

New York City

"I still can't believe you did this." I must've said the same thing two or three times already, but CT didn't comment on the repetition.

"I won't be upset if you change your mind about making such a huge commitment so quickly," he said suddenly, stopping on the top step and turning to face me. "I meant what I said before about waiting until you were ready."

I moved up next to him to make it easier for me to meet his eyes. He needed to see that I meant every word I said. "And I meant it when I said I'd marry you as soon as we could get in front of a judge." I gave him a wry smile. "I just didn't realize that you had the sort of connections to pull this off so quickly."

"Never doubt a Hunter when it comes to getting something he wants." He wrapped his arms around my waist and pulled me close. "And I want you. Forever."

"Forever's a long time," I warned him.

His eyes darkened, and his voice was rough as he spoke, "And it still won't be long enough."

A thrill went through me, and I pushed up on my toes to meet his kiss partway. His mouth met mine, and everything else faded away. No icy wind or bone-chilling cold could reach me. The din of the city that never slept faded. I could have been in any place, in any time, and only he would have mattered.

When the kiss ended, his forehead rested against mine, our mingled breathing puffing white as we simply appreciated being here with each other.

"I never thought something like this was possible," he said quietly. "The way I feel about you. The way I feel when I'm with you. It's almost like it's..."

His voice trailed off, as if he couldn't find the words to properly express how he felt.

I had the words though. "It's too big to be real."

He chuckled, a low sound that stirred things low in my belly. "Exactly."

We stayed where we were for a few minutes longer,

then broke apart with similar sighs. He took my hand, lacing his fingers between mine, and we walked into the courthouse together. My heeled boots clicked against the floor, echoing through the nearly-empty building. The day after Christmas wasn't a federal holiday, but with Christmas in the middle of the week, a lot of judges had postponed trials until the following week, which meant the usual bustle of plaintiffs and defendants, prosecutors and defense attorneys had been drastically reduced. At least that was what CT had told me when he'd announced this morning that we were going to get married that same afternoon.

I'd thought he was joking at first, but then he'd produced a marriage certificate and told me to meet him at two o'clock.

"Are you sure you don't want a big church wedding?" CT asked for the third time. "I don't want you to regret this."

"I won't," I promised him and squeezed his hand between mine. "I've never imagined a big, fancy wedding. All I've ever wanted is someone who loved me enough to make a sincere commitment to a life together."

That was the sort of sentence that would've sent another man running. All CT did was smile and lean over to kiss my temple, confirming what I already knew. I couldn't explain it, but I knew this was exactly where I was supposed to be and who I was supposed to be with. The flutter of nerves I was currently experiencing was excitement and anticipation rather than anxiety.

Except in one particular area.

"What about you?" I asked, finding the courage to finally ask the one question that had been circling my mind from the moment the shock of his proposal had lessened. "Are you sure you don't want to wait until your parents are on board with this?"

He shook his head. "They need to see this as my decision and respect it. I can't say how long that will take, and I don't intend to wait around while they get used to the idea of me making another decision I didn't consult them about."

I tugged on his hand, bringing him to a stop. "You're not doing this just to rebel against them, are you?"

His eyes widened. "No, I swear. I love you, and I want to marry you. I–"

I pressed my fingers to his lips, stilling them. "I don't doubt your feelings. I know those are genuine, and so was your proposal. I meant the timing. I want to make sure you're not trying to rush into things because you know your parents won't approve."

He bit the pad of my finger, then kissed it, his tongue flicking over the sting. "No," he said firmly. "This is me wanting to start our life together as soon as possible."

I searched his expression, his eyes. I believed him with everything inside me. "All right then." I nodded and exhaled a long breath. "Let's go."

Less than fifteen minutes later, we stood in front of a tall, thin woman who CT had said had been one of the first women judges in this district. He'd done a piece on her for his school paper, and they'd spent some time talking during various functions. She was known to be objective...and discreet.

The ring CT slid on my finger was a simple gold band that matched the one I'd given him a minute ago. I didn't have an engagement ring – not really necessary when the wedding came barely twenty-four hours after the proposal – but I didn't mind the lack of adornment. These rings had belonged to CT's maternal grandparents, and he'd inherited them a few years ago. The way he talked about them told me all I needed to know. They'd been important to him, which meant the rings were important to me. I didn't care about their price tag.

"...You may kiss the bride."

The twinkle in CT's eyes made me think he was going to do something crazy and embarrassing, but his kiss was brief and almost-chaste. Still, it warmed me to the core.

"Congratulations, Mr. Hunter," the judge said with a smile. "Mrs. Hunter."

Mrs. Hunter.

I was a Mrs.

Holy shit. I was married.

We'd really done it.

"If you'll sign the license, I'll make sure it's properly filed," she said, pointing at the paper on her desk. She then looked over my head to the two people I'd completely forgotten about. "I need your signatures where it says *witnesses*."

Witnesses had been the one thing CT hadn't thought of. He said that if he'd remembered, he would've told Finn and Griselda to come, but since we were already at the courthouse and didn't want to wait, he'd grabbed the first two people he'd seen and asked for a favor. Sandra Claude, the wife of a public defender who'd forgotten his lunch, and Jerry Lawrence, a janitor who'd done this twice before, stepped up to the desk to take care of their side of things.

Once everything was signed and all congratulations given, CT and I found ourselves standing outside the judge's chambers, feeling like we'd just been through a whirlwind, and both struck by the knowledge that the two of us had completely turned our lives upside-down.

"I need to sit down," I said, making my way over to a bench. My head was spinning, my knees weak.

"You aren't regretting this already, are you?" CT sat next to me, true concern on his face.

"No," I assured him. "It just hit me how much this is going to change everything. School. Financial aid. Where I live. Where you live. Where *we* live."

He put his hands on either side of my face. "It's okay. We'll figure it out."

"Your parents will want us to have a pre-nup," I said. "They're going to think I'm with you only because of the money and they'll never believe otherwise. Or they'll think I'm pregnant and I tricked you into marrying me so that—"

He kissed me, effectively shutting me up. His mouth moved against mine with single-minded determination until I forgot everything, including my new name.

"Now," he said as he ended the kiss, "let's not get ahead of ourselves."

I blinked at him, my mind still too befuddled to process much of anything.

"I want us to share each other's lives. Everything. That includes any and all money I have access to. I trust you, Abigail Slade Hunter. With my life and my heart. No reservations."

A swell of love rose up in me. "Have I mentioned how much I love you?"

His entire face lit up. "Tell me again. Always tell me."

I leaned forward to give him a light kiss. "I love you. Always."

"And I love you. Always."

I kissed him again before sharing my newest concern. "I just know we'll have to put up with people telling us we're moving too fast, that this isn't a good idea. My family, probably. Your family, definitely. I don't think anyone will understand."

"I have a suggestion," he said as he reached over to tuck some hair behind my ear. "Let's not give anyone the chance to ruin this. We deserve time to be happy, to figure out what we want our life together to be before we give our families the chance to weigh in."

"You don't want to tell our families?" I asked. I didn't believe for a moment that he was ashamed or anything like that. I simply wanted clarification about what he was suggesting.

"Not about us being married," he said, his eyes scanning my face, clearly searching for a reaction. "Not yet. Let them think we're dating. My parents are going back to Boston tomorrow. Your parents aren't in New York either. We can live together here, build our marriage the way we want, and we can decide when we tell people and how."

The idea had appeal. I wasn't in the best place with my family right now, and I didn't even want to think about what it'd be like to try to explain all this to them. I had no doubt that telling the Hunters wouldn't go over well, and I didn't want to be responsible for driving a wedge between CT and his parents. We wanted this to be forever, and family came as a part of that.

"I'm not saying I don't want people to know we're married," he said, pressing his lips to my forehead. "If you want, we'll go rent out a billboard right now."

"No." I shook my head. "I like the idea of waiting to tell our families. Maybe once they see how good we are together, they'll start suggesting we get married."

He chuckled. "Then we can tell them that we're already married, enjoy the look of shock on their faces."

I laughed and leaned my head against his strong shoulder. "Or we never tell them and go through whatever big ceremony everyone expects us to have. Let them all have their fun, and we get to keep a little secret just for ourselves."

"I like that idea." He brushed the back of his hand down my cheek. "Something no one else gets to have."

I took his hand between both of mine. "As long as we make our decisions together, I'm happy. I don't want to be like my parents, getting into fights they could have avoided if they'd just talked to each other."

He raised my hands and kissed my knuckles. "I promise you, we'll always talk. About the things that matter, and the things that don't."

After a moment of silence, I asked, "What's next?"

He grinned and stood, pulling me to my feet. "Our honeymoon, of course."

That surprised me. "A honeymoon? How did you manage to pull that off?"

"I know someone who knows someone," he said cryptically. "What do you think about renting a cabin in the woods for a few days? It could end up being another one of our special things..."

TWENTY-THREE
JAX

AFTERNOON, DECEMBER 25TH, PRESENT DAY

Hudson Valley, New York

"'...and so I came up here to the cabin alone, knowing your grandfather wouldn't be able to bear learning about the secrets your parents had kept.'" Blake's voice was rough as he continued to read the letter Grandma Olive had left in the firebox. "'I don't blame them for not telling us that they had married so quickly, and I believe they must have had good reasons, maybe even the ones I suggested. I wish this wasn't how you boys found out any of this, but if I would have been there to talk to you, then this letter would've been destroyed long ago. I can only ask that you forgive me and your grandfather, for not having the strength to talk to you about your parents. To tell you about them, about how much they loved all of you and wanted to see you grow up."

He stopped, his hands shaking, and I reached over to take the letter from him. There wasn't much left for me to finish, which was good because I wasn't sure if I could've read more than a few sentences.

"'The loss of Chester, Abigail, and Aimee reminded me of how unpredictable the world is, which is why I've made arrangements to ensure that, if something happens to me, what I wasn't able to share with you boys won't be lost. Never forget that even if your grandfather doesn't say it often, we both love you all very much. Grandma Olive.'"

I set the letter back on the table in case one of the others wanted to read it, then put my arm around Syll. She leaned against me, neither of us saying anything. Knowing that my parents had secretly gotten married six months before the anniversary date we'd always been told wasn't earth-shattering. Knowing that they'd been working toward buying this cabin for our family and had wanted to keep it a secret for a while longer hadn't changed the way I thought of them.

It was hearing about how their story had begun that had my heart aching. They had to have been so hopeful. Their lives stretched out in front of them. Planning for children, grandchildren. They'd had no idea how little time they actually had.

"There's one more thing in the lockbox," Blake said. "A safety deposit box key. With a note that says, 'more stories about your parents.'"

I didn't need a mirror to know that my face wore the same sort of gob-smacked expression that my brothers wore. After Grandfather had died, we'd written off ever learning anything new about our parents.

All because our grandparents hurt too much to talk to us. Or to each other, apparently.

I wasn't going to be like that.

"I don't know about the rest of you," I said, "but I think Syll and I could use some time alone."

She looked surprised, but judging by the expressions on my brothers' faces, they were grateful for the suggestion. Something told me that I wasn't the only one who'd gotten something important out of Grandma Olive's letter. None of us said anything else as we went our own ways.

I managed to wait until Syll closed the bedroom door behind her, but that was as long as I was willing to go.

"I'm scared," I blurted out. The confession should have made me feel foolish, but if anything, it took a huge weight off my shoulders.

"Scared?" Syll took a step forward and took hold of my hands. "Of what?"

I saw only concern and love on her face, heard only warmth in her voice, and it prompted me to keep going. "I don't want to become my grandfather. I don't want to stop talking with the people I love because I'm worried it'll hurt."

"Are you afraid that...that *I'll* hurt you?" She looked appalled.

"I'm afraid you'll someday get tired of dealing with me and realize you can do so much better."

She gave me a strange look. "Is that why you've been working all the time? Why you changed the things I was doing at *Pothos* so I was in the office instead of with you?"

I linked her fingers through mine, holding on tight. "I thought that if you spent less time with me, it'd take longer for you to...leave."

She stared at me. "You idiot."

"Um, okay?"

She let go of my hands and poked my chest. "I thought you were working all the time because you'd realized that you didn't want to be married to me and you were just waiting until after the holidays to tell me."

My jaw dropped. "Syll, I love you. Why would you think that?"

She poked me again. "Well, for one reason, you haven't wanted to have sex with me in weeks."

I wrapped my hand around the back of her neck and hauled her to me, intending to kiss us both breathless. When her tongue flicked out first, I met it with my own, twisted them together, then moaned as she wrapped her arms around my waist, her hands dropping to grab my ass.

Damn, I'd missed her.

When my lungs burned, I finally released her mouth, barely managing to keep both of us on our feet.

"I always want to have sex with you," I said hoarsely. "It just didn't feel right, mauling you the little bit of time we spent together. I never wanted you to feel like sex was the only reason I wanted you."

She laughed, shaking her head. "Jax, I've wanted you to 'maul' me since the first time I met you."

"If I remember correctly, you slammed the door in my face."

"Because it was either that or drag you inside and fuck you on the bar."

I groaned, that mental image seared into my head. We'd had sex in the bar before it'd burned down, but not nearly often enough for my imagination. Now, I was picturing what it would've been like to stretch out on the bar and have Syll ride me to oblivion.

"I've been scared too."

Her words brought me back, and I wrapped my arms around her, going cold at the thought of how close I could've come to losing her if it hadn't been for Grandma Olive's letter verbally knocking some sense into me.

"Scared of what, sweetheart?"

She tipped her head back to look at me. "I wanted to talk to you about starting a family, but I didn't want you to think I was rushing things. And then you started working late, and it made me wonder if you'd even want that. Even wanted–"

"I do," I cut in before she could say anything else. "I want a family with you. And I want a different life than my grandparents had. A different one than my parents had. I want us to talk to each other. You, me, my brothers, Cheyenne, Addison, and Brea. I want us all to stop hiding things."

Syll reached up and wrapped her arms around my neck. "Then there's something else I need to tell you."

"Okay."

"I don't want to live in our house anymore."

I hadn't seen that coming. "All right. Any particular reason why?"

"I feel like it has ghosts for you. Not just from when you were a kid, but from being an adult too. I think you've kept it more out of obligation than anything else, and if we're going to have a family of our own, I want to raise them someplace warm. Not just a house, but a home. A real home."

I nodded. "First thing tomorrow, I'll talk to my brothers and ask if any of them want it. Who knows, maybe Slade and Cheyenne will decide that it'll be easier to have Estrada move in with them here."

"Especially if my suspicions about Cheyenne are right." Syll gave me a knowing smile.

"Your suspicions?"

"I think she's pregnant." When I opened my mouth, Syll put her finger on my lips. "I don't think she's told Slade yet, so let's keep that to ourselves."

I nodded. "Besides, it's been a long time since my wife and I have had some quality time together."

"It has," she agreed, her voice sinking lower.

"And I'm thinking she might need me to remind her who's in charge."

Syll gave me a saucy wink and took a couple steps back, her hands playing with the hem of her shirt. "That depends. Are you going to let me take a more hands-on role at the club?"

I narrowed my eyes, stalking toward her. "I don't like the idea of anyone ogling my wife, and if you're there, people will ogle."

"Did you ever think that maybe I don't like people ogling my husband?" she countered. "You are entirely too fuckable for your own good."

Her compliment startled a laugh out of me. Her shirt hitting me in the face cut it off.

"You know," she continued as if she wasn't standing there in a mouth-wateringly sheer black bra, "if we worked together in the club, it would make it much easier for the two of us to sneak into the playrooms. Lots of prime baby-making time."

The thought of her walking around the club, sans panties, my cum dripping down her thighs, my baby growing in her belly...fuck. We could take our time later. I needed to be in her.

Right.

Fucking.

Now.

Always.

TWENTY-FOUR

CAI

AFTERNOON, DECEMBER 25TH, PRESENT DAY

Hudson Valley, New York

I had memories of my parents, of us as a whole family. I had memories of my grandparents before the crash and how they'd been with all of us. Now, I wondered how much of that was colored by grief.

I wasn't under any illusions that any of the people I loved were perfect but finding out that my parents had felt the need to hide the depth of their connection from Grandfather and Grandma Olive had shifted my perspective on all of it. We all knew about Grandfather and Dad butting heads over Dad's decision not to take over the family business, but I hadn't realized how deep that division had run.

I finally understood what had driven Grandfather to

alter his will, forcing his grandsons to finally address the issues between us. Seeing how far apart we'd grown reminded him too much of how things had still been between he and Dad when Dad died. He didn't want us to be that way, to have those regrets.

It was his final gift to us.

Grandma Olive hadn't wanted it either. She'd kept this place for us, made sure we'd be able to know our parents, even if she was gone. I liked to think that if she'd lived a few more years, she would've brought us here herself, told us these things then. Without her, it was up to us to ensure that our family's memories were preserved.

That was her final gift, and I couldn't let it be wasted.

I needed to talk to Addison.

I couldn't go another day without telling her how I felt. It wouldn't be fair to either of us for me to be reluctant or have doubts when it came to having kids. It wouldn't be fair to the kids.

As the others went their own ways, I stood and held out a hand to Addison. I didn't want to go back to our room. It'd be too easy to lose myself in her, to forget about all of this. Later, after we talked, I could allow it, but right now, I needed to be strong for us both.

I led her into the kitchen, memories of our earlier

tryst here flooding my mind. Judging by the flush to her fair skin, she was thinking the same. I swallowed a groan of frustration. Not at her but at myself for the lack of control I had around her. I was a Dom, one who thrived on control and being in charge, not just of my sub's body, but of my own.

Around Addison, however, I found myself back to those embarrassing days of adolescence where a rush of hormones could turn a walk down the hall into torture. Back then, I'd quickly learned that I could focus my mind on facts and figures to lock down those seemingly uncontrollable responses. As I'd aged, my control had only grown...until I met her. Then, all bets were off. There were times when it took every ounce of self-control I possessed not to have her up against a wall or bent over a piece of furniture, everything and everyone else be damned.

"Do you want something to drink?" I asked. "I think there's some eggnog left over. Or I could make cocoa."

She brought me over to the table, her expression serious. "I'm thinking we need something with a higher alcohol content. Let me."

I nodded mutely as I took a seat. I didn't know whether to be grateful that she seemed ready to talk about things or terrified that she'd already made up her mind about what she wanted, and I wouldn't be able to handle it.

I watched her as she rummaged around in the kitchen, gathering ingredients. Tall and slender, with surprising strength in her lean muscles, she looked like she could've been a ballerina. When she wasn't thinking about what she was doing, I could believe it too. Her problem was how often her mind got too far ahead of her feet, and her limbs forgot essentially everything they knew about grace and balance.

"One of the family traditions that my stepdad brought in when he married my mom was something he called his Noddy Toddy. Essentially, it was whatever rum we had left over from the 'grown-up' eggnog, plus honey and spices until he liked the taste of it."

She brought two mugs to the table, setting one in front of me and taking the other for herself as she sat down. I took a drink, and the liquid warmed me straight down to my toes.

"That's really good," I said, aware of how lame my compliment was, but unable to think of anything except what I knew I needed to tell her. I steeled myself and jumped right in. "Grandma Olive made a good point in her letter. We all need to communicate with the people we love if we want to have healthy relationships."

"I agree."

"There's something I have to tell you, and I'm asking that you let me get through it before you say anything."

The expression on her face was grim, but she nodded.

"Ever since we got the results back from the doctor, we haven't talked about what the next step's going to be. I know most people assume we'll go the medical route. We're scientists, after all, and we understand better than most what all this would entail. And if that's what you want to do, I'll support you one hundred percent. I'll go to every appointment, be with you whenever and wherever you need me."

Her eyes glistened as I spilled out my heart to her. "Oh, Cai. I–"

Keeping my eyes on her face, I held up a hand, needing to continue. I needed to push myself onward to the true heart of the matter.

"But I'm absolutely petrified of you doing all of that. I know, logically, that you'd be one of the lowest risk women getting these tests and procedures, but I feel like even a fraction of that percentage is too high a risk just to have a biological child. At least for me. DNA doesn't matter to me. If it does to you, I'll accept and support that, but I needed you to know where I stand."

A look of such relief washed over her face that I felt my own trepidation ease.

"I don't want to do all of those tests and everything else that might be involved," she said after clearing her throat. Her hands were wrapped so tightly around her mug that I feared she might break it. "They might be great for other women but being pregnant has never been the appeal to me. For me, it's having a family, and I don't need to physically give birth to be a part of that. I was so worried that you needed a biological child. Someone to carry on the family name who was blood-related to you. To your parents."

I reached across the table and covered her hand with mine. "Not at all. I don't care how we have kids. I just want to be a family with you."

I sent up a silent thanks to my grandma. If she hadn't left that letter, who knew how long it would've taken me to get my head out of my ass and talk to Addison.

"There are so many kids out there who need families," she said, letting go of the mug to link her fingers through mine. "We wouldn't even necessarily need to look for a baby. "

"That's true." I nodded, excitement growing as we began to plan. "As soon as we get back home, we'll make some calls, see what needs to be done to start the adoption process."

Addison's eyes slid away from mine, a shadow of something crossing her face. "Gene and Sandra were telling me that some people who place their children for adoption actually go through a book of prospective parents and they can choose who they want to raise their child."

Gene and Sandra. Right. I'd almost forgotten about them.

Of course, Addison would be thinking about the announcement they'd made at Thanksgiving. That Sandra was pregnant, and they'd be giving the baby up for adoption. I hadn't asked her about that after we'd gotten the news from the doctor about Addison's condition, and she hadn't said anything, but it had to have hurt her, seeing her brother accidentally getting something that she wouldn't be able to have, and then finding out they were giving...

"What would you think about adopting their baby?"

The question flew out of my mouth before I had the chance to fully think things through, which wasn't really like me at all. I started to take it back, but then my brain finally registered that Addison's face was shining.

"Do you really mean that?" she asked, hope clinging to every word. "I mean, I know you wouldn't joke about something like that, but I've been trying to work up the courage to suggest exactly that same thing, so it's a little unnerving to hear you say what I'm thinking. Not that it should really surprise me. We've always been on the same wavelength. It's more like I'm afraid I'm just hearing what I want to hear because I've been hoping you'd agree to at least talk to–"

"You're babbling, Little Red." I said it softly, but it was enough for her mouth to snap closed. "And yes, I really mean it. When we get back home, I'll make some calls."

She came over to me and threw her arms around my neck. I pulled her onto my lap, pressing my face against the side of her throat. It'd been killing me, holding back from her what I was thinking and feeling. She was the only person I'd ever let in so completely, and losing that, even for such a short period of time, had been like missing a part of myself.

"There is one thing we should probably do before the baby's born," she said, her breath hot against my skin.

"What's that?" I slipped my hand under the back of her shirt and placed my palm on the soft skin of her back.

"Get married."

I raised my head. "Did you just propose to me?"

A grin played at the corners of her mouth. "I suppose I did."

"I'm pretty sure I was supposed to do that."

She laughed. "Well, it was taking you forever to get around to it. And you haven't answered yet."

It was my turn to laugh. "Yes, Little Red, I'll marry you." I stood up, lifting her as I went. "Now, what do you say we find something to occupy ourselves with until we can give the others our news."

"Yes, please...Sir."

TWENTY-FIVE
SLADE

Afternoon, December 25TH*, Present Day*
Hudson Valley, New York

Normally, if my brothers and I had gone into bedrooms with our lovers, it was a sure bet that we'd all be in for hours of kinky, mind-blowing sex. Today, however, I wondered if any of us even had sex on our minds. Granted, I had a feeling none of us could be around our women very long without thinking about fucking them, but if the other couples were anything like me and Cheyenne right now, there were things we needed to discuss before we could get to anything else.

The box still in my socks was at the forefront of my mind as I closed the bedroom door. I had no doubt that I wanted to marry Chey, but I wasn't ready to get the box out yet. I needed to talk to her first, see where we were headed.

I didn't, however, get a chance.

"I have to tell you something." Cheyenne's face was pale.

My stomach dropped. "Are you sick?"

She shook her head. "Not sick." She twisted her fingers together, shifting her weight from one foot to the other.

"Talk to me, Chey." I grabbed her hands. "You're freaking me out."

"I'm pregnant."

I stared at her, her words ringing in my ears. Then they sank in, and I picked her up, covering her mouth with mine before she could do more than squeak in surprise. I dug my fingers into her hair, twisting the soft strands even as I dropped my other hand down to her ass. Her legs went around my waist, and she returned the kiss with an enthusiasm that told me everything I needed to know.

When I finally sat down on the bed, our mouths parted, but Chey stayed on my lap, straddling my waist. I cupped her face between my hands, my thumbs running along her kiss-swollen bottom lip.

"I'm guessing that means you're happy?"

"I am," I promised. "I know we have some things to

figure out to make this work more smoothly, but we can do it. I know we can be happy. You, me, Austin, and..." I reached down between us and placed my hand on her stomach. "When?"

"I think the end of August, beginning of September?" She put her hand on mine. "I haven't known very long. I wouldn't have gotten my nipples pierced if I'd known."

I brushed my lips across hers. "Well, I'm glad I had a chance to play with them before you have to put them away."

"This doesn't mean we have to stop–"

I kissed her again. "We have plenty of time to figure out what this means for our sex life. Trust me, Chey, that's not my priority. *You* are. You and Austin." Damn emotion burned at my sinuses. "And our child."

"I love you." She leaned in for another kiss.

I couldn't think of a better time. "Will you marry me?"

She sat back, her eyes wide. "You don't have to do that just because–"

"Get the pair of black socks from my suitcase." I smiled at her. "Trust me."

As she did what I asked, I stood and followed her. I watched as she unrolled the socks and found the small box I'd hidden there. She looked at me, then at the box.

"I've been trying to figure out the best way to ask if this is what you want. If you think this is too fast."

She opened the box, her breath catching at the sight of the diamond and emerald engagement ring I'd bought the day after we'd moved to Boston. I took the ring out of the box and held it up.

"Cheyenne Lamont, I love you, and I want to spend the rest of my life with you. I want to be your husband, and a father to Austin," my smiled stretched so wide that it hurt, "and all of the children we'll have together. Will you marry me?"

Her eyes glistened with tears as she nodded. "Yes." It came out in a whisper, but it was steady.

I slipped the ring on her finger, then raised her hand to kiss her knuckles. "We'll work out the details when we get home. I was already thinking that we could look into getting a bigger place, somewhere Estrada could live too, but with her own space. She can watch Austin and help out with the new baby as much as she can. If we have to get extra help, we will. If you still want to enroll in fall classes—"

"Slade." The humor in her voice caught my attention. "You're babbling as much as Addison."

As the two of us laughed together, I caught a glimpse of what my future would be like with this woman at my side. Warmth and joy, life and love. We'd have Austin and this baby, and more. My brothers and their families. I would finally have everything I'd ever wanted and never thought I'd have.

I picked Cheyenne up again and carried her over to the bed, prepared to spend the rest of the day showing my fiancée how much I loved the idea of being her husband, and being a father.

TWENTY-SIX

BLAKE

Afternoon, December 25th, Present Day

Hudson Valley, New York

I didn't think twice about taking Brea's hand and heading out the back door. I'd gone out this way to get the tree and found a passable, and absolutely beautiful, path through the woods. I'd already been planning to take Brea for a walk the next time I felt the walls closing in. It seemed as good of a place as any to talk.

It was funny. A year ago, the idea of talking to anyone would've had me looking for the nearest exit. Hell, I wouldn't have even been here a year ago. I'd been happy living on my ranch in Wyoming...or so I'd thought. Brea had changed my whole world, and I knew that if I wanted her to stay, I had to keep growing, because ring and baby or not, she wouldn't accept anything less than my best.

I wouldn't accept anything less for her.

"It's beautiful here." We'd been walking for nearly fifteen minutes before she broke the silence. "Do you think you and your brothers will keep the cabin, now that you know the story behind it?"

"If they don't want all of us to share it, I'm going to buy it," I said. I hadn't even realized I'd made the decision until I spoke. Not wanting her to think I wasn't considering her opinion in the matter, I added, "Unless you don't want to."

She smiled at me, then stepped a few feet ahead of me and threw her head back, eyes closed as delicate flakes landed on her nose, her mouth, her eyelashes.

"How could I not want this?"

I watched her, wondering – not for the first time – where her peace came from. Any that I had, I knew, came from her, but she always had more to give.

"Tell me what you want," I said. "Now. Tomorrow. Ten years from now."

She opened her eyes and looked at me, understanding written on her face. "You want to know if you're going to be enough."

She turned to me and took my hands. We both wore

gloves, but it didn't matter. I knew her body as well as my own.

"I've been wondering the same thing about me," she admitted, startling me.

"Brea, you're everything." I squeezed her hands. "If I don't say it enough, then I'll do better because you should never doubt that marrying you and having a family with you is everything I wanted, even when I thought I didn't."

Her face lit up as she smiled, and she reached up to wrap her arms around my neck, pulling me down for a kiss. The wind was cold against my cheeks, but her mouth was warm and pliable as my tongue stroked inside. I was barely aware I was walking her backward until she came up against a tree. Icy fingers chilled my skin as they tucked under the waistband of my pants, and it took me a moment to realize what she was doing.

"Are you crazy?" I growled the question. "It's freezing out here."

She gave me a pout that she only ever used for one thing, and it'd been too fucking long since I'd seen it.

"Warm me up, Blake," she said as she shoved her hand down the front of my pants.

I yelped as her chilled skin came in contact with something very sensitive of mine. My erection flagged, but then her fingers wrapped around my cock, and I let out a guttural curse.

"Please, Blake. I want you to take me out here, on this beautiful Christmas Day."

One stroke. Two. Three. Fuck. Her thumb swept over the tip.

"Don't you want to make this a Christmas tradition?" She worked her hand faster over my dick. "A quickie out here in the woods?"

Shit. If she kept going like this, I was going to cream in my pants.

Before I could stop her, her hand was gone, and my eyes flew open. "What the fuck, Brea?"

She grinned as she turned around to face the massive pine tree behind her. With a coy wink thrown over her shoulder, she unsnapped her pants and pulled them down low enough that I could see the moisture on her pussy.

"This is going to be fast," I warned her.

"It's okay," she said. "I've been wound so tight these last few days, I'll probably come as soon as you're inside."

"You do that," I said as I pushed my own pants down far enough to free my throbbing cock. "And feel free to scream my name. Might as well set the standard for my brothers."

Her laugh turned into a cry of pleasure as I entered her with one smooth stroke. She didn't come immediately, but it only took two more thrusts before she was moaning and shaking, her entire body shuddering with the force of her orgasm. I'd seen many beautiful things in my life, but none of them could compare to watching this woman climax.

"Almost there." I moved harder against her, the thin grip I'd had on my control completely slipping.

"Yes, yes, yes, yes," she chanted, reaffirming that she was enjoying this as much as I was.

I'd forgotten how good we were together, how well we knew each other's desires. She pushed back against me, forcing me deeper to the point where I knew she was getting some pain with her pleasure. And then she was coming again, this time with my name on her lips. My hips jerked, and that was it. Spots danced behind my eyes, and I dug my fingers into her hips as my world went white.

When I came back to myself, I was wrapped around Brea, still half-hard inside her, both of us held up by the tree. We would need to save clean-up for back at the cabin and getting back quickly was a good idea. As much as I'd enjoyed this, I didn't want to risk frostbite.

I smiled as I realized that frostbite was now my top concern. Not Brea tiring of me, not of her thinking I wasn't enough. We'd get married as planned and have our baby. My brothers and I would continue to mend fences, and next year, we'd all come to the cabin for Christmas. This time, Austin and Estrada would have to come too. It would be, after all, a family affair.

Well, everything except the walk I planned to take Brea on after everyone opened their presents. That'd be just for the two of us.

THE END

A Legal Affair Box Set

The Client

Indecent Encounter

Dom X Box Set

Unlawful Attraction Box Set

Chasing Perfection Box Set

Blindfold Box Set

Club Prive Box Set

The Pleasure Series Box Set

Exotic Desires Box Set

Casual Encounter Box Set

Sinful Desires Box Set

Twisted Affair Box Set

Serving HIM Box Set

Pure Lust Box Set

ABOUT THE AUTHOR

M. S. Parker is a USA Today Bestselling author and the author of over fifty spicy romance series and novels.

Living part-time in Las Vegas, part-time on Maui, she enjoys sitting by the pool with her laptop writing her next spicy romance.

Growing up all she wanted to be was a dancer, actor and author. So far only the latter has come true but M. S. Parker hasn't retired her dancing shoes just yet. She is still waiting for the call to appear on Dancing With The Stars.

When M. S. isn't writing, she can usually be found reading– oops, scratch that! She is always writing.

For more information:
www.msparker.com
msparkerbooks@gmail.com

ACKNOWLEDGMENTS

First, I would like to thank all of my readers. Without you, my books would not exist. I truly appreciate each and every one of you.

A big THANK YOU goes out to all the Facebook fans, street team, beta readers, and advanced reviewers. You are a HUGE part of the success of all my series.

Also thank you to my editor Lynette, my proofreader Nancy, and my wonderful cover designer, Sinisa. You make my ideas and writing look so good.

Printed in Great Britain
by Amazon

87685253R00124